Allhallow's Eve

Richard Laymon

headline

Copyright © 1985 Richard Laymon

The right of Richard Laymon to be identified as the Author of
the Work has been asserted by him in accordance with the
Copyright, Designs and Patents Act 1988.

First published in 1986
by New English Library

First published in this new edition in 1994
by HEADLINE BOOK PUBLISHING

A HEADLINE FEATURE paperback

15

ISBN 978 0 7472 4783 8

Typeset by Keyboard Services, Luton, Beds

Printed and bound in Great Britain by
CPI Antony Rowe, Chippenham, Wiltshire

HEADLINE BOOK PUBLISHING
A division of Hodder Headline PLC
338 Euston Road
London NW1 3BH

Allhallow's Eve

1

Clara Hayes had lived alone in the last house on Oakhurst Road ever since a heart attack struck her husband at the top of the stairs and he tumbled down to land at her feet. Dr Harris said the broken neck killed him before cardiac arrest got the chance. That was eleven years ago.

He'd been a cranky old bastard, and she was well rid of him.

Alfred was a far better companion than her husband had been, even though Alfred spent most of the day stalking through the cemetery behind the house.

The ten o'clock news came on, so Clara knew it was time for Alfred to come in. She used her remote to turn off the television, then picked up her cane and hobbled out to the kitchen. She opened the back door.

A chilly wind blew against her. She took a deep breath of the fresh October air, and peered across her yard.

'Al-l-l-fred!' she called.

Generally, she would hear the clink of his collar tags before ever seeing him. She listened, but heard only the dry shuffling of leaves on the graveyard trees.

'Al-l-l-fred?'

Careful not to fall – her broken hip last year had laid her up good and proper for five months – she stepped down the three wooden stairs to the yard. She made her way across the moonlit lawn, and stopped at the edge of her flower bed. From there, she peered through the bars of the cemetery fence. So dark over there, the trees shading the moon.

'Al-l-l-l-fred!' she called. Much too loudly. She imagined heads rising in their coffins, turning – corpses listening to her voice. Softly, she called, 'Here, kitty-kitty-kitty.'

Her eyes searched the darkness.

Saw a solitary figure near the cemetery fence.

Gasping, she took a quick step backwards. Her foot slipped on the dewy grass. She jabbed down her cane, and caught her balance.

'Dear me,' she muttered.

She looked again at the dark figure – the stone angel of a monument she'd seen thousands of times before, in daylight. The graveyard looked so different at night. She didn't like it, not one bit. She should've stayed in the doorway to call Alfred, the way she always did after dark.

'You just stay out,' she muttered, 'if that's your drother.'

She turned away from the cemetery, and started her journey back to the open kitchen door. She hurried. The back of her neck tingled with gooseflesh, and she knew it wasn't the wind's doing.

I'm just being silly, she thought. That graveyard's safe as apple pie. I'm just letting my jitters get the best of me.

Never yet been a corpse crawl out of its hole and go chasing after live folks. It's not hardly about to start happening tonight.

Fur brushed her leg, and she yelped.

Alfred scampered up the porch steps, stopped abruptly in the doorway, and looked over his shoulder at Clara.

'You rascal,' she said,

She took a deep, shaky breath, and pressed a hand to her chest.

'Scared my wits out,' she told him.

She started to climb the steps.

That's when she heard a quiet, muffled clank rather like a crowbar dropping onto a wooden floor. Staring at Alfred, she hardly breathed.

The cat turned away, as if bored. He disappeared into the kitchen. Clara hurried in after him. She swung the kitchen door shut, and locked it.

Alfred sat down in front of the refrigerator. He looked back at Clara.

'Not just now,' Clara whispered.

Turning off the kitchen light, she limped into the dining room. She made her way past her highboy. The room was dark, but she saw no use in planting herself smack in front of the window where she just might be seen – so she approached the window from its side.

If she just had one of those cardboard periscopes like Willy used to play with ... Well, you couldn't ever see much with that contraption, anyhow.

Bracing herself on the cane, she leaned toward the window. She eased aside the soft, priscilla curtains and peered out.

The Sherwood house, next door, looked no different

from usual. The old colonial was just as dreary and forlorn as could be: its driveway and lawn overgrown, its siding sadly in need of paint, its windows boarded over.

Though she couldn't see its front door from here, she knew it was padlocked shut. So was the back door. Glendon Morley, the real estate man, had the only keys.

Maybe he'd gone in, for some reason. Didn't seem likely, though. He hadn't come by with house-hunters since July, and Clara suspected he'd given up on trying to foist off the place. Who'd want to live there, after what happened?

If it wasn't Glendon in the house, though, who could it be?

Maybe some kids broke in. They'd done that once, a couple years back, and run around hooting and howling like a bunch of banshees.

She'd rung up Dexter, that night, and he'd gone in and rounded them up and brought them out in cuffs.

Clara frowned. She hated to bother him at this hour, just to send him on a wild-goose chase. Could be the noise she'd heard didn't come from the Sherwood house at all.

She'd swear it did, though.

And she knew she wouldn't get a wink of sleep, knowing someone was inside that grim old house, wandering its dark rooms, and probably up to no good.

Might even be the killer, himself. They never did find out who did away with all those Sherwoods. Maybe he came back, after all these years...

She got the shivers, just thinking about it.

'Well.' She sighed.

Letting the curtain fall, she stepped away from the window. She hobbled out of the darkness and into the comforting lights of her living room. Lowering herself to the couch, she picked up the telephone. She placed it on her lap and dialed 0. As she listened to the ringing, Alfred sprang onto the couch and nuzzled her arm.

'Directory assistance,' said a flat voice.

'Put me through to Dexter Boyanski, on Jefferson Street.'

'What city, please?'

'Ashburg.'

She scratched Alfred's neck. He purred loudly.

'That's 432-6891.'

'I'm blind,' she lied. 'Would you dial that for me?'

'Certainly.'

Moments later, she heard quiet ringing. Then Dexter's voice. 'Yes?' he asked.

'Dexter, this is Clara Hayes.'

'How *are* you?'

She laughed softly. 'I'm still in working order, thank you.'

'Well, that's mighty good to hear. Betty says you haven't been to bingo lately.'

'Nor will I, long as Winky Simms is calling. He calls so slow, I grow moss in my ears just waiting on him. Why they let him keep on is more than I can fathom – the poor man stutters like a scratched record.'

'Well...'

'Anyway, that's not why I called. I was out back calling in my cat, a while ago, and I heard some noise in the old Sherwood house. Now, I had a long look at the place. It appears just as dead as always – but then, you can't tell much from looking 'cause it's all boarded up. I'm not up to snooping around to see if it's still locked, but I'll wager it's not. Dexter, there's somebody in that house.'

'I'll come out and have a look.'

'I think you'd best.'

Dexter, having just finished a shower when Clara phoned, was wearing his bathrobe. Since he had to get dressed, anyway, he decided he might as well put on his uniform.

Too chancy, doing police work in civvies.

As he dressed, he thought about calling the station. Either of the men on night shift could handle this as well as him. Clara was an old friend, though. If she wanted Chet or Berney, she would've called the station. She was probably hoping he'd drop in, afterwards, and chat a spell.

Dexter got into his Dingo boots. He hurried out the front door, strapping on his gunbelt, and ran to his car.

When Clara heard an engine, she went to the side window of her living room and looked out. A car turned into the driveway of the Sherwood house. It wasn't a white police car with a rack of lights on top, like she expected, but a big man in uniform and a Stetson climbed out. He turned toward her and raised a hand in greeting. So it was Dexter, all right. She waved back, and he turned away.

She watched him stride through the knee-deep weeds. He climbed the porch steps, vanished briefly behind the pillars of the veranda, and reappeared for a moment before entering the recess that hid the front door from her view.

He wasn't out of sight for more than a moment before he stepped back and trotted down the stairs again.

He walked toward her, shaking his head. At the corner, he turned and walked along the side of the house.

Face close to the glass, Clara watched Dexter until he turned the corner.

It'll take him a bit to check the back door, she thought. If it's locked proper, he'll probably go around the other side of the house to the front, and then come over and say, 'She's locked up tight as a drum, Clara.'

'I know I heard something.'

'Well, maybe it came from the Horners' place.'

Gazing out the window, she suddenly hoped the noise *had* come from the Horner house. She hated to think of Dexter finding the back door broken open, and walking into that dark house where such awful things had happened.

She wished, now, that she hadn't called him.

Could've phoned the station house instead, and they'd have sent out one of those other cops. Wouldn't matter so much, a different cop going in that dark old house.

They weren't her friends.

Wouldn't matter, so much, if they never came out.

The padlock was fastened in place, but four screws were missing from the latch plate on the back door. Dexter turned the knob. He pushed the door open.

Unholstering his revolver, he looked into the kitchen.

He shined his flashlight in. It lit the linoleum floor, the closed door to the hallway, the gap where the refrigerator used to be.

And he remembered that other night, so long ago. The refrigerator's white door smudged with bloody handprints. Hester Sherwood's handprints. She must've staggered into the kitchen hoping to get a weapon. Half-dead already. Bracing herself against the refrigerator, leaving those grotesque, three-fingered prints with her right hand. They'd found her severed fingers upstairs, on the bedroom carpet. Somehow, she got this far before the killer caught up to her. Just far enough to leave those deformed prints on the refrigerator, before he threw her down and did the rest.

Suddenly, Dexter didn't want to enter the house. He didn't want to take those two or three steps, and look at the place on the floor where they'd found Hester.

Found her naked.

He'd danced with her once, at the prom they'd both chaperoned a year before the killings. Held her in his arms. Felt the push of her stiffly-brassièred breasts against his chest. All of her encased under the soft gown, armored to protect her skin from touch. She even wore white gloves to her elbows.

There on the floor, armor gone. Flesh laid open, breasts...

Quickly, to stop remembering, he stepped into the kitchen. He swept the flashlight past the cupboards, stove, sink. Refused to look at the floor. Hurried into the hall.

It used to be carpeted with a plush, red runner. Now the hardwood floor was bare. He opened a door to his left, and entered the dining room. He shined his light on the wall where kids had painted their names, a couple of years ago. The names remained, 'John + Kitty', circled by a heart. Innocent, out of place in this crypt of a house.

Dexter suddenly noticed splashes of red on top of the painted heart.

He raised his flashlight up the wall, and groaned.

Who the hell?

Someone had painted a large hand above the heart – a hand dripping blood from the stubs of two severed fingers. The paint glistened in Dexter's light. He stepped close to the wall. Clamping the flashlight between his thighs, he raised a hand and touched the paint.

Still wet.

He grabbed the flashlight and spun around, shining it on the other walls, the ceiling. No more murals, thank God.

The guy who did this, though – the sick bastard who painted the hand – he might still be inside the house.

Dexter rushed across the empty room. The double doors to the foyer stood open. He stepped through them, sweeping his light from the front door to the living room entrance, and up the stairway on his right.

He'd leave upstairs till last, he decided.

Silently, he stepped past the banister. He looked down the narrow hallway that led back toward the kitchen. Then he crossed it and entered the living room.

His light cut through the darkness in a quick circle as he pivoted. Nobody in the room but him.

Something didn't belong, though.

Propped against the wall.

He walked toward it, uncertain what he was seeing. It looked like a cage, or . . .

I'll be damned, he thought.

Window grates. Half a dozen of them leaning against the wall.

Somebody – maybe Glendon Morley – must be planning to fix the place up. Take the boards off the windows. Put up the wrought-iron bars, instead, to keep the vandals out.

Raising his light, he saw that grates were already in place on the living room's three side windows.

On the inside though.

What kind of fool . . .?

Behind Dexter, a floorboard creaked.

He spun around, gasped, and raised his pistol.

Clara, still bent and peering out her window, was so worried she could hardly bear it.

Dexter must've found the house open, just as she'd feared. Otherwise, he would've shown up long ago.

He's in there, this very second. Even with her eyes wide open, Clara could imagine him climbing those long, dark stairs, going into the very bedroom where they'd found James Sherwood with his eyes carved out – so they say. The real story never did come out, but she guessed that most of what she heard was true. Poor Dexter. Why, she wouldn't set foot in that house for a million dollars.

Bad enough, just living next door. She'd have moved away, long ago, if she'd had the money to spare.

How could he go in there? Well, it was her fault. She'd asked him to.

Damnation, she wished she'd rung up the station house instead of Dexter.

Oh, thank goodness!

She breathed a deep, shaky sigh of relief as she saw him walk around the far end of the veranda.

Nobody in tow.

Must've been a false alarm, after all. What took him so long, though? He must've found the back door open, and gone in to search the place. Whoever made that noise probably ran off before Dexter got there. Either that, or hid real good. She didn't much like the idea of *that*.

He waved to her.

Clara gestured for him to come on over.

He nodded, his Stetson tipping forward, and Clara left the window. She hobbled across the living room, opened the front door, and stepped halfway out to hold open the screen for him.

Dexter walked slowly through the darkness, his head down.

'Didn't find him, huh?' she asked.

Dexter didn't answer. He didn't look up.

'Dexter, what's wrong?'

He shook his head.

As he climbed the porch stairs, Clara reached to the wall and flicked on the overhead light.

Blood! All over his uniform shirt and trousers as if a bucketful had been dumped on his head.

'Oh my Lord!' Clara gasped. She covered her mouth.

Dexter took off his Stetson and grinned at her. For an instant, she thought he'd put on a Halloween mask to scare the daylights out of her. Then she knew it wasn't a mask. It wasn't Dexter at all, inside that blood-soaked uniform.

A bare foot kicked her cane away.

With a tiny gasp, she fell against the man. He flung her inside the house.

Her head smacked the floor.

Whimpering, she opened her eyes.

The front door swung shut, and the man stood above her.

2

Eric Prince woke up, that night, with a straining bladder. He climbed from bed, and made his way to the shut door.

A straight-backed chair was propped under its knob, a precaution he always took when he went to bed in the deserted house. Though fifteen, and too old to be afraid of staying alone, he liked the secure feeling that came from having his door barred.

As he removed it, he wondered vaguely if his mother was home yet. He had no idea what time it might be. When he opened his door, though, he saw that the hall light was still on.

Mom would've turned it off.

She must still be out. Eric's worry came back, the same worry that fluttered in his stomach every time Mom went out on a date – that he would wake up, in the morning, and she would still be gone. He'd wait and wait, but she would never come back.

Maybe she had run away with a handsome stranger she met in a bar. Eric would get a postcard, a week later, from a distant city.

Or she'd been killed in a car accident.

Or the worst of all – a worry that started after he read an old paperback called *Looking for Mr Goodbar* – she'd met a terrible man on one of her dates, and he had slaughtered her.

Chief Boyanski would come to the house. 'Son, I'm afraid I've got some bad news for you.'

Then Eric would be alone. An orphan. Nobody, in all the world, to take care of him. Maybe he could be like *The Little Girl Who Lived Down The Lane*, and stay alone in the house...

These thoughts upset him, driving his grogginess away so that he was completely awake when he pulled open the bathroom door and saw a naked man urinating. Eric jumped back, yelling. The startled man flinched.

Eric ran for his room, clenching his muscles to keep his own pee inside. He was almost to the door when his mother stepped into the hall.

She blinked in the brightness, and tied the belt of her threadbare flannel robe. Her hair was mussed. She looked confused. 'Eric, what're you doing up?'

'There's a *man* in the john!'

'Oh. That's only Sam.' She smiled sadly. 'He must've given you quite a scare, huh?'

Eric nodded.

Down the hall, the toilet flushed.

'Sounds like he'll be right out,' Mom said.

'Who is he?'

'A friend.'

She's naked under that robe.

Eric looked away from her. 'Night,' he said, and went

14

into his room. He shut the door and stood in the darkness.

'Damn,' he heard a man say. 'I'm sorry about that.'

'It's okay,' said Mom. She sounded depressed. 'Something like this was bound to happen, sooner or later.'

He heard them walking away.

'Maybe I'd better leave,' the man said.

'No, don't. Please.'

'Shouldn't you have a talk with him?'

'It'll wait. This wouldn't be a good time, anyway.'

He heard the soft bump of a shutting door. If they were still talking, Eric couldn't hear them.

He opened his door. The hallway was deserted and dark. He walked silently to the bathroom, and locked it in case the man came back. Standing over the toilet, he freed himself and started to urinate.

The man had stood right here, naked, just like he owned the place. And he had such a big *thing*. Had he really been putting it into . . . Sure he had. The thought of it made Eric feel sick, as if he'd swallowed a milkshake too fast.

He flushed the toilet.

He walked back to his bedroom, and opened the door. Without stepping inside, he shut it. The noise sounded loud in the stillness.

As silently as he could, he left the house by the back door. He hurried through the chilly, wet grass alongside the house. Mom's VW in the driveway. A bigger car was parked at the curb.

Eric stared at that car for a long time, wondering about the man who owned it, the man in bed with Mom even at this moment. Fucking her. It sounded so dirty and exciting, like jacking off only a hundred times better. He'd day-dreamed a lot about doing it, and imagined it was the neatest thing in the world especially if the girl was someone beautiful like Miss Bennett, or Aleshia Barnes. Even if the girl wasn't beautiful, it'd be great just getting to see her naked, getting to touch her breasts. He could hardly imagine what it would feel like to touch someone's breasts. They must be *so smooth* . . .

He looked down. His penis was poking erect through his pajama fly. He slid his fingers down it, trembling. Then he quickly covered it. This was no time to get all horny.

He rushed to the VW, and ducked beside it. Peering over the hood, he saw that the windows of Mom's bedroom were dark. He crept to the rear of the VW. Squatting beside it, he looked both ways. The road was clear, and he saw no activity at any of the nearby houses.

No excuse to wait.

He dashed down the driveway to the rear of the other car and ducked behind its trunk. On hands and knees, he dug into the curbside debris. His fingers pushed through soggy leaves, twigs, something slippery that writhed away. And then he found a triangle of glass from a broken bottle.

Just the thing.

Gripping it firmly, he pressed the shard against the

shiny surface of the trunk, and dragged it down. The sound, like fingernails scraping a blackboard, made him cringe. But it didn't make him stop.

He cut a huge X into the top of the trunk. When he finished, he ran a finger along one of the furrows, and smiled.

3

Sam Wyatt woke up. The bedroom was gray and chilly, but under the covers he was warm. Rolling onto his side, he looked at Cynthia. Her eyes were open. She turned her head toward him, and smiled sadly.

'Didn't you sleep?' he asked.

'A little, I guess.'

'Worried about Eric?'

She nodded. 'I feel so damned rotten.' Her voice trembled on the last word, and she pressed her lips tightly together as if fighting not to cry.

Sam put a hand on the hot skin of her belly. Cynthia stroked the back of it.

'You're anything but rotten,' he said. 'You did all you could to keep him...'

'In the dark?'

'Protected.'

'I feel like such a slut.'

Sam started to take his hand away, but she held it.

'No, I don't mean *that*,' she said. 'With you ... I've never felt so happy and alive. And clean. But Eric ... he doesn't know. You're a stranger to him, and he must think his mom's sleeping with a stranger.'

'You can tell him different.'

'I will. I just wish it hadn't happened this way. I mean, what a way for him to meet you.' She shook her head. 'It was supposed to be for his own good, you know? I didn't want him knowing the men I dated – getting attached to them. That happened a couple of times, where he started looking on them as – like father figures. He was just devastated when these men suddenly disappeared from his life. I mean, it's bad enough for an adult when a relationship ends. But for a kid who's never had a father ... I just couldn't put him through that, anymore. It wasn't fair to him. Maybe that was a mistake, I don't know. But I think it saved him from a lot of heartache.'

'Maybe so.'

'Do you think I was wrong?'

'You didn't have to protect him from me. I'm not going to disappear.'

Her eyes went cold. 'No?'

'No.'

'I've heard that before.'

He looked into her accusing eyes. 'Don't blame me for what the others did.'

'I'm not.'

'Because I'm not them, I'm me. It's bothered me for a long time that you didn't want me to meet Eric. I just let it go, but it didn't make me feel good to be kept hidden from him as if you're afraid I'll contaminate him.'

'He would like you, Sam. He'd...' Cynthia's eyes brimmed with tears. 'He'd fall in love with you, just like I did.'

'Would that be so awful?' he asked. He tried to smile, but his mouth trembled.

'Yes,' she said. 'If you ever left him. He's been left so many times before.' She rolled onto her side, crying softly, and Sam took her in his arms.

'I think I'd better stay home with Eric, tonight,' Cynthia said as they walked down the driveway.

A chilly wind was blowing. Sam liked the way it tossed her brown hair.

'I'll tell him about you,' she said.

'Why don't I take you both out to dinner, one of these nights?'

'We'll see.'

Frowning, he stepped to the rear of his car and looked down at a big X scratched into the paint of his trunk. 'For Christsake,' he muttered. He ran a finger down one of the deep grooves.

'That's *terrible*. Did it just happen?'

'I don't know. I haven't seen it before. Somebody must've done it last night.'

'Kids, probably.'

He stepped over to Cynthia's VW, and looked it over. 'At least yours is okay.'

'What kind of creep would do a thing like that?'

Sam shrugged. 'Somebody who recognized my car, probably, I'm not too popular with some of the people in town. I always keep it garaged, at home. My tires got slashed a couple of times when I was leaving it out.'

She stared at the scratches. 'I'm awfully sorry.'

'Well, these things happen. We've got a saying, "If you want to be loved, be a fireman."'

'You think it's because you're a policeman?'

'More than likely. Well, I'd better be on my way.'

'Yeah. It's time for me to wake up Eric.' She stepped into his arms.

He felt her shivering through the frail robe.

'Call me tonight?' she asked.

'Sure.' He kissed her. 'You'd better get inside before you catch pneumonia.'

He stopped at his duplex for a quick shower and shave, then drove to the station. The office was deserted except for Betty on the switchboard. She swiveled around to face him. 'All quiet on the western front,' she announced, smiling.

'*Das ist gut,*' Sam said. He poured himself a cup of coffee, and wished he'd grabbed something from the refrigerator before leaving home: a hunk of cheese, a hot dog. The coffee tasted wonderful. 'Where's Dex?' he asked.

'I would hazard a guess that he's on the way.'

Sam glanced at the clock. 'He's never late.'

'Rarely.' She took a sip from her own coffee mug, and rubbed the lipstick print with her thumb. 'In the twelve years I've spent laboring under his yoke, he's been late only four times. Five, including today.'

'Absent?'

'Six days, four of them the week Thelma left.'

'Hangovers from celebrating?'

'That should've been the case, but it wasn't. To look at him, you'd think the world had ended. Men can be so foolish when it comes to pretty women.'

'You should know.'

'Indeed I do.' At fifty-two, Betty was still a slim, good-looking woman. 'And I'll admit, I've occasionally taken advantage of starry-eyed men. My husband is a perfect example.' She laughed softly. 'But there's absolutely no excuse for a woman to behave like Thelma. Beauty doesn't give one license to abandon common decency. It's a crime the way she treated that man.'

'Speaking of crime...' Sam finished his coffee, and rinsed out the mug. 'I'd better hit the road.'

'Let me just ring up Dexter.'

While she dialed, Sam unlocked the gun cabinet and took out a sawed-off Browning.

'He doesn't answer,' she said.

'I'll head over to his place.'

'Why don't you? I know he's only ten minutes late, but it's so unlike him.'

'I'll check, and let you know.'

'Thanks, Sam.'

As he got into his patrol car, he half expected Dexter's Firebird to swing into the parking lot. It didn't, though, and he found his muscles tightening with worry as he drove out. He couldn't imagine the chief over-sleeping. The big man had been raised on a farm, and often spoke of the built-in alarm clock that woke him at dawn, no matter what.

Car trouble, maybe.

Heart attack, whispered a corner of Sam's mind.

He kept an eye on all the cars he passed, on those parked along the curbs. At a stop sign, he glanced at Ed's Chevron. No Firebird.

For a moment, he wondered if the vandal who

22

scratched the back of his own car had gone to Dexter's house – maybe slashed Dex's tires, or sugared the gas ... That didn't seem likely, but it was possible. A minor-league vendetta against the Ashburg PD?

Finally, easing around a corner, he came into sight of Dexter's house and saw the chief's red Firebird parked in the driveway.

He picked up the radio mike. 'Car Five.'

'Go ahead, Car Five.'

'Chief's car's parked in his driveway. I'll see if he's home, Betty.'

Sam walked up the driveway, giving the Firebird a quick inspection as he passed it. No flat tires, at least. Nothing unusual about its appearance.

He hurried to the front door and rang the bell. Dexter didn't answer. Sam took a deep breath, and realized he was trembling. He jabbed the doorbell button again and again, then swung open the screen door and banged the wood with his knuckles.

What's the use? He's not home.

Or if he is, he's on the floor dead of cardiac arrest. Or he ate his gun. No, Dex wouldn't do that. Or would he? Or did someone break into the house last night, someone with a major-league vendetta?

None of the above, probably.

Sam tried the door knob. It turned.

Thank God. Dex'd blow his stack if I had to break in.

He stepped inside, automatically wiping his feet on the entry rug as he looked around.

'Dexter?' he called. 'Dexter, you here?'

Beside the easy chair, a lamp was on.

Sam rushed through the living room and up a short

hallway to the bedroom. The shades were drawn, the lamp on. It seemed so wrong, in daylight – like the shunned room of an invalid.

The bed was made.

Okay. Whatever happened, it was probably last night before Dex went to bed. Whatever...

'Dexter?' Sam called again.

The house was silent.

He stepped around the end of the bed. He dropped to his knees, and glanced under it. Nothing there except the electric blanket control. He got up, and looked inside the closet. A few pairs of shoes were scattered on the floor, but the old Dingos weren't among them.

He's in uniform, then.

Sam shut the closet door. He wiped his sweaty hands on his pants, took a deep breath, and felt a tightness in his bladder.

Damn, why hadn't he locked the bathroom door, last night? Must've scared the hell out of that poor kid...

He left the bedroom.

He walked down the hall, past the open bathroom door.

Might as well take care of it now.

Stepping into the bathroom, he glimpsed himself in the medicine cabinet mirror. Looked damn edgy. He rubbed his face. He bent down, and lifted the toilet seat, and saw an eyeless face look up at him through the pink water, gray hair floating as if tugged by a strange wind, tongue lolling.

The lid banged down.

Sam backed against a wall, gasping. Hot fluid gushed up his throat. He covered his month. The sink was too far. He jerked open the shower curtain and bent over the tub and his teary eyes looked down on the blur of a split torso, detached arms and legs.

4

The rear doors of the coroner's van were slammed shut. Sam and the other four officers of the Ashburg Police Department stood on the front lawn of Dexter Boyanski's house, silent until the van was out of sight.

Berney Weissman, the assistant chief, took off his silver-rimmed glasses and squeezed the bridge of his nose. 'All right,' he said in a weary voice. 'Let's take a look at what we've got so far.'

'We've got zilch,' said Chet Summers.

During the past two hours, they'd sketched and photographed the crime scene, searched the house, vacuumed the bathroom floor, and lifted two dozen latent prints. Most of the prints on the labeled cards could probably be weeded out later, as belonging to either Dexter or Sam.

'We know it happened last night,' Sam said.

'Between nine and twelve,' Berney added, quoting the coroner's estimate. 'Chet, you go back to the station and check the log book. See if any calls came in that might have a bearing. Go through the whole day, everything till now. Then get in touch with Ethel and George, find out if anything happened that they maybe didn't bother logging.'

Chet nodded, and walked to his car.

'I'll take this side of the street. Sam, you take the other side. Buck, I want you over on Jackson Street – maybe someone behind Dexter's place heard something.'

'A lot of folks'll be at work,' Buck said.

'So we'll come back again tonight. Let's go.'

Sam crossed the street, heading for the corner house. Damn it, he'd spent last night only three blocks from here. After dancing at the Sunset Lounge, they'd driven up Jackson Street to Cynthia's house. At about eleven o'clock. They might just as easily have taken Jefferson instead, and gone right past Dexter's place, maybe seen a strange car parked in front, or heard a noise...

Well, it hadn't happened that way. No use spending brain power on a pile of ifs.

He pressed the doorbell of the corner house, and heard ringing chimes inside. A dog started yipping. From its high-pitched frenzy, he guessed it was a small dog. Probably one of those miniature poodles. He waited a few seconds, then rang the bell again. The dog *yip-yapped* frantically.

Sam wrote the address on his clipboard. Beside the address, he wrote, 'No response – (dog).'

Then he cut across the yard to the front stoop of the next house. He pushed the doorbell. This one buzzed.

A gaunt man in a green jumpsuit opened the door and looked up at Sam like a weasel peering from its hole. The friendly, curious tone of his voice surprised Sam. 'What can I do for you, officer?'

'A crime was committed across the street last night. I'm interviewing everyone on the block. Did you see or hear anything...?'

'At whose place?'

'The Boyanski...'

'Dex? Shitfire! What'd they do to 'im?'

'He was murdered.'

'Dex?' Sorrow and disbelief filled the man's eyes. 'Goddamn.'

'Did you notice anything?'

'What time you say it happened?'

'Between nine and midnight, probably.'

He ran a hand over his thin, gray hair. 'Damn, I wish I had. I was reading in the back room, most of that time. We'd get together over a six-pack, you know. Goddamn.' He rubbed his chin. 'If I was you, I'd take a mighty hard look at what Thelma was doing, last night. You know Thelma?'

Sam shook his head. 'Never met her.'

'Just have a look at what she was up to last night. That's all.'

'You think she killed him?'

'Well, you know she ran off with that bartender, Babe Rawls, from over at the country club. That was five-six years ago. Nearly busted Dex's heart. I told him, though. "Dex," I said, "you can thank your lucky stars you're rid of that gal." Took him a long spell to get over her, but he finally did.'

'I thought she'd moved to Milwaukee.'

'That's what I heard, too. Saw her over at the Food King yesterday afternoon, though.'

'We'll look into it,' Sam said. 'Could I have your name?'

'Charley Dobbs.'

He wrote it on his clipboard. 'Thank you for the help, Mr Dobbs.'

'He was a good man, Dex.'

'Yes.'

'Goddamn.'

The door shut. Next to Charley Dobbs's name, Sam wrote, 'Saw nothing. Thelma in town?' Then he crossed the lawn to the next house. Nobody answered the door. He wrote 'No response' beside the address, and moved on.

This house was directly across the street from Dexter's place. The door opened as he reached toward its bell.

'Officer?' The sleek blonde wore tweed slacks and a white blouse as if dressed for a luncheon – or a visitor.

'My name's Sam Wyatt.'

'I'm Ticia Barnes.' She offered her hand, and he shook it.

'Do you have a couple of minutes, Mrs Barnes?'

'Certainly. Please come in.'

He thanked her, and stepped into the house.

'Would you care for some coffee?'

'No thanks, I just had some.' He followed her into the living room. He could smell the warm odor of coffee, and wanted a cupful. But he preferred to avoid bathrooms. God, he'd never be able to raise a toilet lid without seeing Dexter's head...

'Are you all right?' asked the woman.

He nodded. 'It's been a rough morning.'

'I should imagine.' She sat near the end of the couch, and nodded toward a chair. 'I noticed all the ... activity at Mr Boyanski's house. The coroner was there?'

'Mr Boyanski was killed last night.'

Her lips pursed. She said, 'Ooooh.'

'Did you see or hear anything?'

'No, I'm afraid not. I always draw the curtains at night, and of course it's been too chilly, lately, to leave the windows open. Was Mr Boyanski *murdered*?'

'Yes.'

'How horrid! Right across the street?'

'We're not sure that's where he was killed, but we ... found him there.'

'Dreadful.'

'Was anybody else in the house who might've seen something?'

'My husband's away on business. He's *forever* away. My daughter may have noticed something, though. Her bedroom windows face the street. What time ...? Do you know when it happened?'

'Probably between nine and midnight.'

'Aleshia was in her room, then,' the woman said. 'I hardly ever see her, since we gave her that telephone. So she may very well have noticed something. Of course, she's in school right now. A junior at Hi. She won't get home until – oh – around five, I imagine. Cheerleader practice.'

Sam noted it on his clipboard, and got up. 'I'll drop by this evening, then.'

'Fine. Any time after seven.' She rose. 'Are you certain I can't get you some coffee?'

'I'm certain. Thanks, though.'

They walked toward the door.

'You don't suppose...?' She hesitated. 'I do get nervous, sometimes, being alone so much. Is there any chance... You don't suppose he'll strike again, do you?'

'It's possible. I'd keep my door locked, just in case.'

'We've never had a murder across the street.'

'We don't get many in this town.'

'The fewer the better, as far as I'm concerned.'

'Me, too.' He thanked her.

'We'll be expecting you later, then.'

'Right,' he said, stepping outside.

'Good luck.' With a quick smile, she shut the door.

Sam made notes on his clipboard, then crossed the yard to the next house. He pushed the doorbell button, but didn't hear it ring inside. So he knocked on the aluminum frame of the screen door. A few moments later, the inner door opened.

'Hi Ruthie.'

'Sam?' The hefty woman rubbed an eye with the palm of her hand. She wore a quilted, pink robe and her feet were bare. 'What's up? Some kind of trouble?' She swayed to one side and craned her neck as if to see what might be going on behind him.

'Dexter's been killed. Murdered.'

Her mouth dropped open. 'Oh my *God*.'

'It happened last night, between about nine and twelve. We're going door-to-door to see if anyone noticed anything unusual.'

'Anything unusual,' she muttered. 'I better call Mike. Maybe he...'

Sam shook his head. 'No need to bother him, just now. I'll stop by the store, later on today.'

'I'm going in, soon as I get myself together. I'll tell him to give it some thought. You know, I *did* see something struck me a little strange.'

Sam's pulse quickened.

'I ran out of cigarettes, last night, and remembered I had a pack in the glove compartment. I was right, too. Found half a pack. Anyway, I was heading back to the house and I heard a car start up. It was Dexter's car. He pulled out of his driveway and headed up the road real fast. I remember thinking he must've got some kind of emergency call.'

'What time was that?'

She frowned. Her tongue pushed against her cheek, bulging out the pale skin as if a nervous animal were trapped in her mouth and trying to burst out. 'During the news,' she finally said. 'The ten o'clock news. I was waiting around for that silly sports announcer to come on – the one that looks like a chipmunk? He didn't come on till almost the end, and that's when I made a beeline outside to fetch my cigarettes. So I guess it must've been around ten twenty-five.'

Sam wrote it down. 'Which way did Dexter go?' he asked.

Ruthie nodded to her left. 'He went speeding up that way, and turned left on Third Street. His tires squealed, he took the corner so fast.' Her tongue made a knob in her cheek again, and she shook her head. 'Wherever he went, he was in a big rush.'

5

'You rat on me, I'll cut your dick off. You understand?'
Nate pushed his face close to Eric's. Though only
sixteen, the boy had dark whiskers like someone much
older. He also had breath that made Eric think of dead
snakes baking in the sun. 'You understand, fag?'

'I'm not a fag.'

'Oh yeah? Coulda fooled me.'

'You've got my money. Why don't you just leave me
alone?'

''Cause you're a wimpy little fag, shitface.'

He spat on Eric's face, and grinned. Eric gagged at the
sweet smell of the dripping saliva. With a laugh, Nate
shoved him against a urinal.

'Thanks for the loan, fag.' Nate left.

Still gagging, Eric hurried to a sink. He splashed
water on his face, then scrubbed it with the grainy pink
soap powder. After rinsing, he thought he could still
smell Nate's spit. He gagged again, and once more
scoured his face.

The bathroom door swung open.

'Prince!'

He recognized the voice of Mr Doons, the vice
principal. Quickly, he splashed water onto his face.

33

'Prince, what're you doing in here? Have you got a pass?'

'No sir.'

'What're you doing out of class?'

He reached for the paper towel dispenser. 'I came in between periods, Mr Doons.'

'What are you, deaf? The bell rang five minutes ago.'

'I'm sorry.'

'Sorry doesn't cut it, Prince. When're you gonna shape up?'

Eric rubbed his face with the rough, brown paper.

'Answer me.'

'What do you want me to say?' he asked, his voice trembling. He swallowed. He didn't want to cry, especially not in front of Mr Doons.

'You've got a crappy attitude, Prince.'

'What'd I *do?*'

The v.p. stabbed a blunt finger at the floor. 'Give me thirty push-ups, Prince.'

'That isn't fair.'

'*Now.*'

Eric lowered his eyes. The tile was spattered with water – or worse. 'The floor's wet.'

'Do it!'

'There's piss on the floor!' His voice cracked, and tears flooded his eyes.

Doons smiled. 'It'll do you good, Prince.'

Eric crouched, and placed his hands on the gritty floor. The tile under his left hand was wet. Crying silently, he started doing push-ups.

'Let's hear it.'

'Three, four, five . . .'

'All the way down, Prince.'

'Six, seven . . .'

'Louder.'

'Eight.'

'I can't hear you.'

'Nine, ten, eleven . . .'

'Think you're real smart, don't you?'

'No.'

'Gonna cut class again?'

'No.'

'Gonna wise off?'

'No.'

'Gonna put another dead rat in Miss Major's deck?'

'No.' So *that was it!* 'Twenty-three.'

'Thought that was smart, didn't you?'

'No.'

'Made her puke.'

'Twenty-eight,' he said, no longer crying as he remembered the way she barfed. It had served the bitch right.

'Twenty-nine, thirty.' He quickly dried his eyes as he stood up.

'That was a sick, perverted thing you did to her, Prince.'

Eric lowered his eyes. He'd thought, at the time, that he'd been let off too easily. He decided that Miss Major was too embarrassed by the incident to tell the administration. She wouldn't want her own part to come out.

Apparently, he'd been wrong.

She'd told some of it, at least. To Doons. Not all of it, though.

She certainly couldn't tell the reason Eric put the rat in her desk. She wouldn't dare.

'Do you want to know why I did it?'

''Cause you're a sick little wise-ass. Now get to class.'

Eric turned to the sink.

'No time for that. Get going. And next time you step out of line, Prince, you're gonna wish you hadn't.'

'Yes, sir.'

Eric left the bathroom. Doons followed him, a few steps behind, as he walked up the hallway. He opened the door to his English class, and entered.

Miss Bennett glanced at him. There was no malice in her eyes. She continued talking about Huck Finn.

Eric hurried to his seat. The rat had been worthwhile, if only because it got him transferred to Miss Bennett's class. He liked her a lot. She was pretty – so pretty that he often got horny just looking at her – and she never put him down.

He watched her talk. Her blue eyes were shiny and intense. She held a paperback copy of *Huckleberry Finn* in one hand. Her other hand gestured, pointed to students for answers, and sometimes brushed aside the blond hair over her forehead.

Eric's own hair hung down, tickling his right eyebrow. He wanted to push it into place, but Doons hadn't let him wash his hands. He didn't dare touch himself.

God, what a crud.

Doons and Nate both.

They're probably pals.

Eric used the back of his wrist to shove the hair away. He rubbed his eyebrow.

'Eric?' asked Miss Bennett.

'What?'

'Do you have something to contribute?'

'Uh, no.' He blushed. 'I was just scratching.'

The class laughed.

God, what a day!

When the period finally ended, he rushed to the bathroom and washed his hands. No matter how much he scrubbed, he still felt they were dirty.

He went without lunch because he had no money to buy it.

The rest of the day, his stomach felt empty and he was careful to keep his hands away from his face.

Finally, the last period ended. He walked home alone, and opened the mailbox. Quickly, he flipped through the envelopes. One neatly typed envelope was addressed to him.

Unlocking the door, he hurried into the house. He tossed the other mail onto a lamp table. With a trembling hand, he tore open his letter.

He pulled out the single sheet of paper, and unfolded it.

JOIN THE FUN
SPOOK-HOUSE HALLOWEEN PARTY!!!
THRILLS, GAMES, PRIZES, REFRESHMENTS!!!
COME IN COSTUME – BRING A FRIEND
TO THE BIGGEST, BEST
SCARIEST!!
HALLOWEEN PARTY EVER
WHEN? OCTOBER 31, 9 PM

**WHERE? THE OLD SHERWOOD HOUSE
823 OAKHURST ROAD**
DON'T MISS OUT!!!

6

Martin Bodine, proprietor of Marty's Motor Lodge, scowled at the photo. 'Not here,' he said.

'The picture's six or seven years old,' Sam told him.

'Still not here.' He pushed the photo back across the registration desk. 'Sorry,' he said. He didn't look sorry.

'*Has* she been here?'

'When?'

'Within the past week.'

'No.'

'She could look different, now. A different hair style or color ...'

Martin sighed. 'I've got twenty rooms, *Mister* Wyatt. As of right now, fourteen of 'em are vacant. That means I've got six parties under my roof. You think I wouldn't know it, if this gal was one of them? Let me tell you, I'd know it. She's not here. She wasn't here last night, or the night before. As far as I know, I've never seen the gal my whole life. All right?'

'All right,' Sam said. 'Thanks for your help.'

'Any time.'

Sam walked to the door, clamping the photo of Thelma to his clipboard. Marty's Motor Lodge was the second motel he'd checked after searching Dexter's house and finding a picture of the ex-wife. He'd struck out at both. There were no more motels to try – not in Ashburg. Maybe she'd taken up lodgings in one of the neighboring towns, but Sam doubted it. More likely, she was staying with a friend.

He climbed into his patrol car and drove to the Food King, where Charlie Dobbs had spotted Thelma yesterday. Outside its doors was a pile of pumpkins. Sam remembered buying one only a few days ago. He'd planned to carve a jack-o'-lantern this evening. Now, he doubted he would get to it. He wondered if Cynthia had a pumpkin. It would be fun, getting together with her and Eric to make jack-o'-lanterns. Maybe next year, he thought, hurting with regret.

Inside the store, he found the crew-cut manager behind a booth, okaying a woman's check. He waited until the woman left.

The manager beamed at him. 'Yes?'

'I'm looking for information about a customer who was in here yesterday,' he said, and handed over the photo. 'Do you recall seeing her?'

'Mmm. Say, isn't this Thelma Boyanski?'

Sam nodded.

'You say she was here?'

'That's what I heard.'

'Golly, I haven't seen her for years. Back in town, is she?'

'Apparently.'

'What a gal. I always wondered what happened to her. She used to be in here two-three times a week. Ran off with Babe Rawls, last I heard. Come back, has she?

Well, doesn't surprise me. She was a dope to step out on a guy like Dex. Must've finally come to her senses.'

'You didn't see her yesterday, though?'

'Nope. But I keep pretty busy. Could've missed her in all the rush.'

'Okay if I talk to your clerks?'

'Help yourself.' He gestured for Sam to follow. They went through a closed checkout aisle. Near the back of the store, a young man was stamping new prices onto coffee cans. 'Paul, Officer Wyatt wants to ask you a few questions.'

Paul blushed. His chin was pitted and raw with acne.

Sam showed him the picture, and asked the question.

Paul looked as if he wanted to faint with relief. Sam wondered, briefly, what the clerk had done to cause such guilty responses. Probably nothing more than an illegal U-turn a week ago.

'I don't think I've ever seen her in here,' Paul said.

'Have you seen her someplace else?'

'I don't think so.'

'Okay, thanks.'

The manager squinted at Paul, and turned away. They walked down the aisle. 'Wonder what that boy's got on his conscience?'

'Hard to say,' Sam said.

'You see how he looked? He looked as guilty as Judas. Like he thought you'd put him under arrest. I wonder if maybe he hasn't been taking home some merchandise in his pockets.'

'Could be. Plenty of folks do. I wouldn't suspect him, though, just because he got flustered. We've all done things we're ashamed of, and wouldn't want the police to know about.'

'Think I'll keep on eye on him, just in case.'

Half a dozen people waited in the 'Express Line.' Sam smiled at two of the women he recognized. Then he turned his eyes to the manager, who was speaking quietly to the checkout girl. The 'girl' was pushing fifty. She had a lean, tough look. She glanced at Sam, one eye squinting, and nodded. She mouthed a silent, 'Over here.'

They left the manager at the cash register, and stepped over to his deserted booth.

'What's your pleasure?' she asked. Her voice wasn't low and harsh, as Sam expected. It was a high-pitched, musical voice.

'I'm looking for this woman.' He gave her the photo.

'Oh?'

'I heard she was in here yesterday.'

'She most surely was,' lilted the clerk. Her plastic nametag read, 'Louanne.'

'You saw her?'

'With my own eyes. She didn't look exactly this way. Wears her hair up, now, and it's more a dishwater color. Thinner, too. But I saw her, no mistake about that.'

'Did she go through your line?'

'Oh yes.'

'Did she pay with a check?'

Louanne fingered her upper lip. 'No, not with a check.'

'She paid cash?'

The clerk grinned. 'Didn't do that, either. You'll never guess.'

'I give up.'

Her eyes sparkled. 'This lady didn't pay for her groceries, at all. I saw a man slip the money into her hand while they stood in line. He did it just as slippery as you please, sneaking it to her 'cause he didn't want nobody spying. I just happened to see him, though. I like to keep my eyes open.'

'Do you know who the man was?'

'I surely do. And it seems mighty strange for a good-looker like this gal to run around with a toad like him.'

'A toad?'

'It was Elmer Cantwell.'

'Elmer *Cant*well?' An odd match, all right. 'That's hard to believe.'

'I had to pinch myself, but it was him all right.'

7

'Come *on*,' Nate said.

'Where to?'

'You coming, or you just gonna stand there with your fist up your ass?'

'Sure.' Bill Kearny slammed his locker shut. 'Where we going?'

'You'll see.'

They walked together up the deserted hallway, their sneakers squeaking loudly on the linoleum. Ahead of them, a classroom door opened. Miss Bennett stepped out. Setting down a stack of books and file folders, she glanced at Nate and Bill. She smiled a quick greeting, then turned away to lock her door.

Bill grinned at Nate.

Nate wiggled his heavy eyebrows, and rubbed his hands together.

They passed Miss Bennett, and turned a corner.

'*There's* one teacher I wouldn't kick out of bed,' Bill said.

'Yeah? I'll take Nelson any time. You seen the tits on Nelson?'

'Nelson's a cow.'

'Yeah,' Nate said. 'Great udders. Let me at 'em!

44

Wouldn't mind Bennett, either, though. Get her alone sometime, you know, and slip her the ol' dick.'

'Do you think she does it?'

'Fucks? Bennett? Are you kidding? A gal that looks like her? She probably bangs her brains out every night and twice on weekends.'

'She wouldn't do it with a kid, though.'

'Who's a kid?'

'Us.'

'Hey, maybe I'm just sixteen, but I've got a major league bat. A regular Louisville Slugger, man, and I hit a homer every time I get up.'

They trotted down a staircase to the first floor, and nearly collided with Mr Doons. They dodged away from him, and kept on walking.

'Whoa there. Houlder, Kearny, back up.'

They came toward him, shrugging and grinning.

'What're you two doing in the halls?'

'We're on our way out,' Nate said.

'Sixth period ended twenty minutes ago. What've you been up to?'

Bill lowered his eyes, as if ashamed. 'I had to stay after for Mr Fredricks.'

'What about you, Houlder?'

'I was helping Miss Bennett.'

'Helping her how?'

'Washing desks.'

'I'll just bet.'

'Yeah. You should've seen what they wrote on those desks.' Nate grinned. 'Lots about you, you better believe.'

'That so?' He glared at Nate.

45

'Very complimentary.'

'I'll just bet.'

'Wanta hear one?'

'Wanta tell me one?'

'Sure, but you gotta promise not to bust me. I mean, I'm not the guy saying it. I'm just reporting what some other kid wrote on a desk.'

'I understand that.'

'And you promise you won't bust me?'

Doons nodded. Bill didn't like the man's narrow, challenging eyes. 'Go ahead.'

'Don't,' Bill said. 'Come on, let's go.'

'I want to hear it,' Doons insisted.

'Okay. Here goes. One said, "Doons eats poons."'

His lips curled up. 'How clever.'

'And one said...'

'Come on, Nate.'

'"Doons sucks Miss Major."'

The man's face burned red. His nostrils quivered. 'Cute,' he muttered. His arms were stiff at his sides, his fists tight. 'One of these days, Houlder, somebody's gonna take you apart.'

Nate grinned as Doons took a step toward him. 'I was only reporting...'

Doons's straight arm barely moved from his side, but his fist knocked into Nate's groin. Nate grunted. He doubled over, clutching himself.

'What's wrong with Houlder?' Doons frowned at Bill as if perplexed. 'Looks like your buddy hurt himself, Kearny.' Laughing softly, he stepped into his office and shut the door.

Nate grabbed the edge of the drinking fountain to

hold himself up. Words squeezed through his clenched teeth. 'Stinkin' rotten no-good mother-fuckin'...'

'Can you walk?' Bill asked.

Nate groaned as he unbent himself. He scowled at the closed door of Doons's office. 'Cocksuckin' fag!'

'Shhh.'

'Let him hear.'

'Come on, Nate.'

He took a step, and grimaced. 'The bastard,' he muttered. 'You don't fuck around with a guy's tool.'

'Let's just get out of here.'

They took a few steps up the hallway. Then Nate turned around. Walking backwards, he yelled, 'Doons eats shit!'

Doons's door swung open.

Nate and Bill dashed up the hallway, the slap of their sneakers echoing. They dodged to the left. Picking up speed, they crashed open the main doors, burst outside, and hurried down the concrete stairs.

They ran along the faculty parking lot.

Miss Bennett, arms loaded, was walking toward them. Apparently, she'd left school by the north wing exit.

Instead of stepping aside to let them pass, she blocked the walkway. 'Slow down, boys,' she said. 'No ru...' Quickly, she sidestepped.

Nate adjusted his course, and plowed into her. She flew backwards, books exploding from her arms. A hedge caught her behind the legs. She tumbled over it. Nate kept running.

Bill stopped.

Miss Bennett lay on her back behind the hedge;

trying to free her upraised legs from the bushes. One of her loafers had come off. She was wearing green knee socks. Bill glanced at her bare thighs, and her pink panties. She quickly flipped her skirt down. Her eyes met Bill's, and he saw they were awash with tears.

'Gee, I'm sorry. Are you okay?'

'No.' She tucked the skirt between her thighs. 'Leave me alone.'

'Here.' He lifted her left foot out of the bushes. Holding it up, he saw that the underside of her leg was scratched and bleeding. He picked up her other foot, and pushed them both sideways. Miss Bennett twisted on her back, and brought her legs down.

'Thank you,' she said in a small voice.

'I'm awfully sorry.'

She stood up. Lifting the rear of her skirt, she looked back at the damage. 'That's a nice friend you've got.'

'He was mad.'

She sniffed, and wiped her eyes dry with the back of her hand. 'Mad, huh?'

'Doons punched him in the nuts.'

Her blue eyes locked into Bill's. 'He what?'

'Doons smashed him right in the balls. With his fist.'

'You're kidding,' she said.

'Honest. That's why Nate was so mad.'

'He was running at a pretty good clip for a guy who'd just been socked in the groin.'

Bill shrugged.

Miss Bennett squatted down, and began to gather the spilled contents of her handbag.

'Here's your shoe,' Bill said, and dropped the loafer over the hedge.

'Thanks.'

While she picked up what had fallen on her side of the bushes, Bill went after the books and file folders along the walkway. He stacked them neatly. Miss Bennett walked around the far end of the hedge, and came up the sidewalk toward him.

She *was* beautiful. Not very old, either – not for a teacher. Maybe twenty-four, twenty-five. As she walked forward, Bill remembered the look of her bare legs. And her pink, nearly-transparent panties.

...slip her the ol' dick.

He felt a warm swelling, and held the books in front of himself to hide the bulge in his jeans.

'I'll take your stuff to your car, if you want,' he said.

'All right. Thank you.'

'You want me to take those?' He nodded toward the four books in her arms, clutched just below her breasts.

'No, I've got 'em.'

They walked, side by side, across the nearly deserted parking lot.

'What's your name?' she asked.

'Bill.'

'Bill what?'

Is she gonna report me? 'Kearny.'

'I'm Miss Bennett.'

'Yeah, I know.'

'Bill, you seem like a pretty nice guy.'

He smiled uncertainly.

...a pretty nice guy, and I'd like to know you better. Why don't you come on home with me...?

Unreal, like one of those dreams. Couldn't happen.

He was right.

'The thing is,' she said, 'you could get messed up if you keep running around with a guy like Nate Houlder. I've heard a lot about him, and none of it's good.'

'He's not so bad.'

Miss Bennett gave him a direct look, then set her books on the roof of a white Omni. He expected her to keep at him, keep hammering the way adults always do. But she said nothing more. She took the keys from her handbag, and opened the car door.

'Well,' Bill said, 'I'll think about it.'

She smiled. 'You get going, now. And thanks for helping me.'

'Oh, you're welcome. I'm just sorry you got hurt.'

He stepped backwards, smiling and nodding. Then he turned away. He crossed the parking lot. At the walkway, he looked around. Miss Bennett, still standing beside her car, was folding a ragged, red towel. She bent into the car, and spread her towel on the seat.

Doesn't want blood on the upholstery, Bill thought.

She looked at him.

Bill nodded, and started walking. He took three steps, glanced back, and saw Miss Bennett quickly lift the rear of her dress before sitting in the car.

That bastard, Nate.

Angry, Bill turned away. He walked toward the end of the building, and Nate stepped out from behind a telephone company van, clapping. 'Hey hey hey, lover boy.'

'She got all scratched up in the bushes.'

'Aww.'

'It's not funny, Nate. You hurt her.'

'Big fuckin' deal. She's a teacher.' He suddenly scowled. 'Hey, you better not've told her my name.'

'I didn't have to.'

'It's tough being a celebrity.' Grinning, he pressed a fist to his forehead and flexed his biceps. 'My reputation doth proceed me. So, Romeo, hows about heading over to my place?'

'I don't know.'

'Got something better to do?'

'No. I'm just a little pissed at you.'

'Yeah? That shows how dumb you are.'

'Oh yeah?'

'Yeah, man, if you had any brains you'd see what a big favor I did for you, blasting Bennett on her ass. I *saw* you looking down at her, her feet in the air. Bet you saw enough to give you wet dreams for a month. You felt up her legs, too.'

'I was helping her.'

'Sure. Helping yourself, too. And kissing up to her like that, you probably impressed the shit out of her. Next thing you know, you'll be slippin' her dick.'

'Shut up, okay?'

'Is that gratitude?'

'You hurt her.'

'But I sure helped you. Now come on, let's head over to my place and grab some suds.'

'Yeah, all right.'

They started walking across the field. Far to their left, the football team was exercising: running in place, suddenly dropping facedown, scrambling to their feet again and pumping their knees until another signal came to drop.

'Assholes,' Nate muttered. 'I could take down any two of those pricks. Blindfolded.'

'Like you did Miss Bennett?'

'You really got a hard-on for her.'

Bill shrugged.

'Tell you what, Billy-my-lad. I'll hold her down, you fuck her.' With a laugh, he shoved Bill sideways and ran. Bill chased him until he was close enough to kick Nate's trailing foot. It tangled with the other foot, and Nate plunged to the ground.

'Aw jeez! Jeez, you've broke me!' Nate grinned, and scurried to his feet.

A magazine in a brown paper cover propped open the lid of the mailbox on Nate's front porch.

'Hey *hey*, it's Dad's *Playboy*.'

He pulled out the magazine, and the rest of the mail. The lid banged shut.

'Here, hang onto this stuff.'

He handed the mail to Bill, then dug into a pocket of his Levis and came up with a key. As he shoved it into the lock, Bill tried to slip the wrapper off the *Playboy*. The magazine bent, the wrapper came free, and Bill dropped half a dozen envelopes.

He bent to pick them up.

'A letter for you,' he announced.

'Yeah? Who's it from?'

Bill checked both sides. He found no return address. 'Doesn't say.' He followed Nate into the house, and handed him the letter.

'Can't be nothin' bad,' Nate said. 'Bad shit's always got a fuckin' letterhead in the corner.'

He tore an end off the envelope, and pulled out a sheet of triple-folded paper. He flipped it open and grinned. 'Well well well, somebody in this armpit of a town has good taste.'

'What is it?'

'An invitation, my man. "Join the fun. Spook-house Halloween Party." Sounds right up my alley.' He scanned the sheet. '"Come in costume." Maybe I'll come as myself, give 'em a treat.'

In Nate's bedroom, they drank two beers each, and looked at the *Playboy*. Nate commented on each picture.

'How'd you like to sink your teeth into one of those?'

'Mmmm, look at that hairy mazoo.'

'Oh hon, suck me off.'

Staring at the photos, listening to Nate, Bill often found himself thinking about Miss Bennett – the way she'd looked on her back, her legs up, her eyes full of tears. He imagined her naked, then felt guilty as if such thoughts were an insult to her.

When he finally got home, late that afternoon, his mother handed him an envelope. 'This came for you today,' she said.

He looked at the envelope, its neatly typed address. He knew, before opening it, what he would find.

'Aren't you going to open it?' asked his mother. She seemed very curious.

'Sure.' He tore the envelope, and pulled out the invitation. The paper was slick and shadowy – the paper of a cheap photocopy machine. He unfolded it. '"Join the fun,"' he read.

'Let me see.'

He gave it to her, and she read it, silently mouthing the words. When she finished, she shook her head. 'Says it's at the old Sherwood house.'

'Yeah. That'll be neat.'

'I don't know, Billy. Don't know if you oughtta be going there. It's a bad place, been deserted fifteen years.'

'You don't believe in ghosts, do you, Mom?'

'It's a bad place, honey.'

8

The Ashburg Public Library was silent, and smelled like furniture polish. Sam walked softly over its carpet.

Behind the circulation desk slouched Elmer Cantwell. More like a bullfrog than a toad. His bulging eyes blinked at Sam.

'May I be of assistance?' Elmer asked in a low voice.

'Is there somewhere private?'

The big head didn't move, but the eyes slid from side to side. 'We seem to be alone. As you may notice, I am presently manning the desk. I can hardly leave my post, can I?'

'Fine.'

'Never fear, I *am* wearing pants and they are zipped. Would you care to see?'

'No thanks.'

'I take it there have been no complaints?'

'Not recently,' Sam told him.

'I shouldn't think so. I have conducted myself with extreme decorum during the past eight months.'

'I'm not here about that.'

'Ah,' Elmer grinned with mild surprise. 'Then what brings you into my presence? Certainly you're not here for a book?'

'That's right. I'm here looking for Thelma.'

'Who?'

Sam held up the photo. 'Thelma Rawls, formerly Boyanski, formerly Connors.'

'Oh, *that* Thelma. I believe she moved to Milwaukee.'

'I believe she's back. Where's she staying, Elmer?'

'I wouldn't have the vaguest notion.'

'Think again. Obstructing a criminal investigation is a lot more serious than jogging around town with your jollies hanging out.'

His slick lips drew back. 'No call to be crude, Officer.'

'You were seen with her. Where's she staying?'

'You might try the Sunset Lounge. That's where I found her.'

'When?'

'Shall we say Tuesday night?'

'Did you leave with her?'

'Yes, I believe so.'

'Where did you go?'

'For a drive.'

'Where?'

'To a quiet, secluded place.' His eyes rolled upward and he smiled. 'Oh, she was just luscious. Would you care for me to recount our exploits?'

'That won't be necessary. Just tell me where you left her.'

'Back at the Sunset Lounge. Her car was there, I believe.'

'Okay. Wednesday. You went to Food King with her. You paid for her groceries. Where did you meet her, where did you take her?'

'We met for lunch at the Oakwood Inn. After shopping, I let her off at the inn's parking lot.'

'Why did you pay for her groceries?'

'Because, Officer, I am a gentleman.'

'Okay. Last night.'

'Yes?'

'Where did you take her?'

'No place at all. I spent the evening at home with Mother. I'm certain she'll be pleased to verify that.'

'I'll check.'

'I know you will. Persistence is such an admirable trait.'

'When did you see Thelma last?'

'Yesterday afternoon, when I dropped her off at the Oakwood Inn.'

'You're sure?'

'Would I lie to you?'

'If I find out you have lied, Elmer, I'll put you in jail.'

'Meany.'

In his patrol car, Sam called the station. Ethel's voice came over the radio. Betty, he realized, had already gone home; the day shift was over.

'Would you look up Elmer Cantwell's home address for me?' he asked.

'Hold on,' said Ethel. Moments later, she gave him the address.

As he drove there, he thought about what he'd learned from Elmer. Thelma had been in town as of Tuesday night, at least. She'd spent some time with Elmer, and made it with him – hard to believe. According to Elmer, they'd been together yesterday afternoon, but not last night. So she didn't have him as an alibi for the time Dexter was murdered.

She still looked good as a suspect.

Looking better all the time.

Sam stopped at Elmer's house. He rang the doorbell a dozen times. Though he felt sure that the mother was home, she didn't answer the door.

Elmer probably phoned, gave her advance warning.

Could Thelma be inside, too? Possible, but not likely. If the rumors were true, Elmer wouldn't want his mother knowing he was involved with another woman.

He rang a few more times, then left and returned to the station.

9

She spooned thick tomato sauce onto Eric's spaghetti. He counted the chunks of Italian sausage, and saw that she was giving him more than usual. Too many chunks to count. He smiled up at her.

'Did you have a good day at school?' she asked.

He thought about his troubles with Nate and Mr Doons. He sure wouldn't tell Mom about that. 'I got invited to a Halloween party,' he said.

'Oh? That sounds nice. When is it?'

'Halloween night.'

She stepped to her side of the kitchen table, and began serving herself. 'Who's having it?'

'Somebody from school.'

'Anyone I know?'

He shook his head. 'It's a costume party.'

'What'll you wear?'

'Haven't decided.'

She sat down. 'Would you like to say grace?'

He lowered his head, and rattled off his memorized prayer. 'Dear God, who giveth us food for the body and truth for the mind, so enlighten and nourish us that we may grow wise and strong to do thy will, Amen.'

'Amen,' she mumbled.

Eric started to stir his spaghetti. 'Are you going out?'

'Tonight? No, I don't think . . .'

'I mean on Halloween.'

She shook her head. 'I'll stay here for the trick-or-treaters, I guess.'

'Will Sam come over?'

He watched her face turn red. 'Sam has to work. He's a policeman.'

'He *is*?'

'He's an awfully nice man, Eric. We've been . . . I've been seeing him for a long time, now. We're very good friends.'

'Oh.'

'He'd like to meet you.'

'I don't want to meet *him*.'

'*Eric.*' She sounded sad. 'He's my *friend*.'

'Must be.' Eric took a bite of sausage, and slowly chewed. It was his favorite meat, but he felt tight inside and he didn't want to swallow.

'I'm sorry you ran into him, that way.'

'Does he come here every night?'

'No. He's only been here a few times.'

'Sneaking around.'

'He does not sneak around. I just didn't want you to meet him, yet, because . . . things don't always turn out and I didn't want you getting attached to him, like you did with John and Raymond.'

He managed to swallow. He pushed at his spaghetti, but didn't take another bite. 'You shouldn't go messing around with men if you aren't married.'

'You don't have to be married to love someone.'

'Then you get kids without fathers.'

'You have a father.'

'Oh yeah? Where is he?'

'He went away.'

'Because he got you pregnant and you weren't married.'

'That isn't why.'

'Then why?'

'He asked me to marry him, but I wouldn't.'

'Why not?'

'Your father wasn't a nice man.'

'Then why did you ... go with him?'

'I didn't.' She stared at her spaghetti. So far, she hadn't taken a single bite. 'He was just a guy in school. We hardly knew each other. He followed me home, one day, and nobody was there but me, and – well, things happened. We were both only sixteen, and ... He got kicked out of school, and got a job at a gas station. He wanted me to marry him, but I just told him no. And then he left town, about a month before you were born, and he never came back.'

'You should've married him.'

'How can you say that? You don't even *know* him.'

'You should've. You should've let me have a dad. It's not fair.'

Her eyes got shiny and her mouth started to tremble. She pushed herself away from the table.

Eric started to cry. She'd made his favorite meal, and now everything was ruined. 'Mom, I'm sorry.'

'Never mind,' she sobbed. 'Just never mind.' She rushed out of the room.

10

Sitting in his car, Sam watched the house. He was across the street, and half a block away. As he watched, he ate a cheeseburger he'd bought at Jack-in-the-Box.

He had arrived at five o'clock, dressed in civvies and driving his own Chrysler. Darkness closed quickly over the street. Lights appeared in the windows of nearby homes. The home of Elmer Cantwell, however, remained dark, and Sam wondered if he'd been wrong about the mother.

At 5:52, light appeared in an upstairs window. It soon went off. A few minutes later, the picture window lit up, and he could see into the living room. Then the draperies slid shut.

He hadn't been wrong about the mother.

At 6:10, a Volvo entered the driveway and stopped. A man climbed out. From his bulging shape and the slouch of his walk, Sam knew it had to be Elmer.

Elmer entered the house, leaving his car in the driveway.

Going out later?

Sam finished his cheeseburger. He turned on the radio, and listened to quiet music. As he waited, a chill seeped through his trouser legs. He had a blanket in the trunk, but didn't want to bother with it. He turned on the car engine. Soon, the heater was blowing warm air on him, and the car began to feel cozy.

Not as cozy as home, though. Nice to be back at his duplex, sitting on the couch, staring at the TV news and sipping a vodka gimlet. Nicer to be with Cynthia. He wouldn't be with her tonight, though, even if this hadn't come up. Maybe she would straighten things out with Eric. It'd be good to know the kid. The three of them could get together, go to movies, go fishing. Not right for a kid to grow up without a father.

Better no father, though, than the guy Eric would've been stuck with if Cynthia'd married that bastard who raped her. Harlan. Scotty Harlan. Damn good thing he'd left town. If Sam ever got his hands on the guy ... Christ, to do a thing like that to Cynthia! She'd cried the night she told Sam about it, cried so hard she could barely talk as she described how he stood with a knife and made her strip, how he pressed the blade to her throat as he took her, and threatened to slice off her nipples if she ever told.

People saw Scotty leave the house, and knew he was the one when she got pregnant, but she never told anyone how it happened. No one but Sam, on a night fifteen years later when he asked about Eric's father and she spoke in a voice so broken by sobs that he cried, himself, and held her tightly.

A guy like Scotty Harlan shouldn't be allowed to live.

Sam had never killed anyone, but he'd like a chance at Harlan.

Maybe not kill him, Sam thought. Maybe just blast

apart his knees. And his elbows. And shove the muzzle against his cock and blow that off.

He realized that he was trembling with rage. He took a deep breath. He wiped his sweaty hands on his trousers.

Keep your mind on the job, he warned himself. No point dwelling on Scotty. You'll never get a chance to do anything about him, never get a chance to stick your gun up his ass ...

Stop it!

Think about Dexter.

Somebody hated Dex awfully bad to cut him up that way, hated him the way I hate Scotty. So who did Dex rape?

He wouldn't.

Berney had Chet and Buck looking through the station files for suspects – guys Dexter had stepped on, over the gears. Guys who might want to return the favor. Even in a town the size of Ashburg, a cop could accumulate plenty of enemies.

Sam put his money on Thelma, though. Former spouse. Showed up in town the day before he was killed. Has to be a connection of some kind. If she didn't handle it herself, she might've put somebody else up to it.

Maybe Elmer.

Even as he thought about the man, he saw Elmer Cantwell leave the house. The hunched figure crossed the lawn and ducked into the Volvo. The car backed out of the driveway.

Sam swung away from the curb, and followed. He stayed a full block behind Elmer's car as it moved up the deserted street. At an intersection ahead, another car pulled in front of him. With this one as a shield, he narrowed the gap. It soon turned onto a driveway. By this time, Elmer was passing the Baptist church. The business district was only a block away. With traffic picking up, Sam didn't bother to drop back. He stayed several car-lengths behind Elmer, and kept moving when the Volvo swung into the parking area of Harney's Liquor.

Near the end of the block, he pulled up to a vacant stretch of curb. He waited, wondering if he was crazy to be tailing Elmer. Tailing him on an *errand*, for Christsake! His old lady probably ran short of apricot brandy ... On the other hand, maybe Elmer planned to do some entertaining.

This could pan out, after all.

Sam chewed on his lower lip, and watched the rearview mirror.

Soon, a car backed onto the road. Sam looked away as it approached. When it passed him, he looked. A Volvo. He let it get a good headstart, then pulled onto the road behind it.

The Volvo approached an intersection.

If he's heading back home, Sam thought, he'll turn here.

He didn't turn.

Sam grinned, and followed. The Volvo led him away from the business district, down tree-shrouded streets. Not far ahead was the entrance to the Ashburg Golf and Tennis Club.

Where Babe Rawls once tended bar.

Where Thelma used to hang out.

But Elmer drove past it.

The open fields of the golf course began. On the other side of the street, the last few houses were left behind, and the cemetery took over.

Sam's headlights lit a wooden sign. 'You are now leaving Ashburg,' it read. 'Come back soon.'

Where the hell's he taking me? Sam wondered.

Better be to Thelma.

11

Eddie Ryker was drying the supper dishes when the telephone rang. His mother lifted a plate out of the sudsy water. 'Would you get that, honey?'

'Sure.' He balled up the dishrag. As he backed away, he shot it toward the sink. It flared out, and dropped like a sheet over the rack of dishes waiting to be dried.

In two long strides, he was at the kitchen door. He picked up the wall phone.

'Hello?'

'Eddie?' asked a soft, breathy voice.

He smiled. 'Oh, hi Aleshia. How are you?'

'I miss you.'

'Me too,' he said, and wished he'd picked up the phone in a different room. He never expected the caller would be Aleshia. She usually phoned much later, talking quietly from her dark bedroom.

'How was football practice?'

'Just fine,' he said. He remembered her waving as she ran by with the other cheerleaders, her legs quick under the pleated skirt. 'How did your practice go?'

'Oh, just fine. Except for Sue. She's such a know-it-all. I just wish she'd fall off her pedestal and break a leg. Or something higher up, if you get my meaning.'

Eddie smiled.

'I suppose you heard about Chief Boyanski?'

'Yeah. It was on the news.'

'Isn't it just ghastly? To think there's a *murderer* running around town! Yick!'

'Well, they'll probably catch him.'

'I hope *so*! It's *disturbing* to have a thing like that, especially the day before Halloween.'

'Well . . .'

'Anyhow, that's not what I called about. I came into a very rude surprise, when I got home from practice.'

'Oh?'

'An invitation came for me in the mails.'

'For that Spook-House Halloween Party?'

'You got one, too?'

'Yeah.'

'Well, do you realize what night that party's scheduled for?'

'Tomorrow night.'

'Precisely.'

'And what else is that night?'

'Your party, of course.'

'Precisely.'

'Well, I wouldn't worry about it. I'm still planning on yours.'

'I should certainly hope so. But what about everyone else?'

'I don't know.'

'I invited a dozen friends to my party. Now suppose

half of them decide they would rather go over to the creepy old Sherwood place? What kind of party'll we have, then?'

'A small one.'

'You may be amused, Edward Ryker, but I most certainly am not.'

'I just don't think it'll happen. Some of the kids you asked might've gotten invitations to the other party, but I'll bet every one of them will decide on yours.'

'Do you think so?' she asked, sounding relieved.

'I'm positive.'

There were a few moments of silence, rare during conversations with Aleshia. 'You don't suppose,' she finally said, 'that somebody concocted this other party just to spite me, do you?'

Eddie laughed. 'Who'd do that?'

'Just about anyone I didn't invite to *my* party, of course.'

'Well, maybe, but I doubt it. I think it's just a coincidence.'

'Maybe yes and maybe no. Anyhow, I have a jillion calls to make. I'll give you a buzz later.'

'Okay.'

'Around ten.'

'Fine.'

'From my bed.'

He grinned. 'Okay, great. Talk to you then.'

'Bye-bye.' She hung up.

'Beth, telephone. It's Aleshia.'

'Right there,' she called to her father. She flipped

through the pages of her physiology book, counting. Six to go in the chapter, but two were mostly diagrams. Not so bad. She could handle that.

She dropped a pencil into the crack of the open book, and got up from her desk. As she stood, she watched herself in the window reflection. The image on the dark glass, transparent as a ghost, hinted of beauty and mystery. It looked good to Beth.

In the reflection, her freckles and braces didn't show.

With a shrug, she turned away. Her eyes avoided the full-length mirror on the closet door: it would show details she didn't want to see.

She hurried down the upstairs hallway, entered her parents' room, and picked up the telephone extension.

'...absolutely marvelous pyramid, and then we all collapse into a pile...'

'I've got it,' Beth said.

'Okie-doke,' said her father. 'Bye now, Aleshia.'

'Bye-bye, Mr Green.'

Beth heard the phone go down. 'Hi-ho,' she said.

'I just adore your father.'

'He's not bad,' Beth said, smiling.

'I only wish *my* father was as cute and charming.'

Beth shrugged. She had never seen Aleshia's father. He seemed to be out of town constantly.

'Anyhow, I just gave you a buzz to find out if you're coming to my Halloween party.'

'Yeah,' she said, confused. She'd already told Aleshia she would be there. 'Is something the matter?'

'It appears that *some*one has decided to go into competition.'

'Oh, you mean the other Halloween party?'

'Precisely.'

'You think it's for real?' Beth asked.

'Why wouldn't it be?'

'It looks awfully queer.'

'Queer?'

'First off, my invitation wasn't signed. It doesn't give the first hint about who's throwing the party, or even ask for an RSVP.' She sat on the edge of the bed, and lay back. 'Second, it's supposed to be at the old Sherwood house. That place has been boarded up for as long as I can remember. How'd they even get in to *have* a party? I just think the whole thing's queer. I bet somebody sent out those invitations for a gag.'

'Or to ruin *my* party.'

'If it is for real, nobody's gonna go. Nobody with sense, anyway. I wouldn't be caught dead in the old Sherwood house myself.'

'Oh, I imagine half the kids in town would love to get in there, especially on Halloween night. It is the creepiest place in the whole world. Wouldn't you like to see where it all happened?'

'No. Thanks anyway.'

'I certainly would, but not when I'm having my own party. I'll just die if nobody shows up 'cause they're all over at the Sherwood house traipsing through gore.'

Beth laughed softly. 'I don't think the gore's still there. Someone must've cleaned it up. I mean, it's been about fifteen years or something.' The hand resting on her flat belly bounced as she laughed. 'And even if it

71

didn't get cleaned up, it'd be all dry, by now. It'd take a putty knife to pry it off the floor.

'Beth! You're awful!'

Beth couldn't stop laughing. Her eyes teared. 'Oh,' she gasped. 'Oh, wouldn't that be a sight...! Some old janitor crawling around with a putty knife ... trying ... trying to jimmy the guts off the floor!'

'Beth, you're sick,' Aleshia said through her own laughter.

'Ohhh. Oh wow.' She wiped her eyes, and tried to catch her breath. 'Oh. Don't know ... what got into me.'

'While you're on that subject, who's your date for the party?'

Beth took a deep, shaky breath. 'I ... I don't know.'

'You *what*?'

'I don't know.'

'Beth, the party's tomorrow night!'

'Oh, I'll find someone to take me.'

'I certainly do hope so. Well, I'd better leave you, now. I've got a jillion more calls to make.'

'Are you phoning everyone you invited?'

'I just might, Beth.'

Karen Bennett sat at the kitchen table of her rented house, correcting a stack of papers turned in yesterday by her fourth period class. She finished Dave Sanderson's Halloween theme. At the bottom, in red ink, she scribbled, 'Cats are people, too.' She flipped to the front page and marked the top B-.

She took a sip of Chablis.

She scooted a bit farther forward, and gently rubbed

the underside of her right leg. Earlier, she'd bandaged the worst of the scratches. For the past hour or so, they'd been feeling itchy. If she used her fingernails, though, they hurt.

That creep, Houlder. She really ought to report him. She couldn't write him up, though, without implicating Bill. She hated to do that.

Hell with it.

She lowered her eyes to the next theme, and moaned. Jim Miller had used a pencil. After all the times she'd told them only to use ink. Doesn't anybody listen, for Christsake? She picked up her red pen.

'Use ink only!' she wrote at the top.

Then she began to read. 'Halloween is the time for tricks and treats. Little kids get dressed up like pirates and hobos and wiches and nurses, and docters and bums...'

The telephone rang.

Thank God.

She put down her pen, picked up her wine glass, and went to the phone. 'Hello?'

'Hello, Miss Bennett. This is Aleshia.'

'Oh, hi Aleshia.'

'I hope I'm not disturbing you.'

'No, not at all. What's up?' Reaching down, she scratched the back of her leg, and winced.

'I'm calling about my Halloween party?'

'Yes. I'm looking forward to it.'

'Oh good. I was a little bit worried that you might change your mind, or something.'

'I've already got my costume ready.'

'Oh, super. I was just wondering, because it turns out

73

there's this other party tomorrow night and I'm afraid some people might decide to go to it instead of mine.'

'Not me.'

'Did you get an invitation to it?'

'No. Yours is the only one I got.'

'Maybe they're not asking teachers.'

'Maybe not.'

'I mean, I didn't invite any, either. Just you. But that's because you're really special, and not like a real teacher.'

'I'm not?' She grinned. 'I hope the Board of Education doesn't find out.'

'I mean, you're a real teacher. You're the best. But you're not like the others. You listen to us, and stuff.'

'Well...' She realized she was blushing. 'Thank you, Aleshia.'

'Do you have a date?'

'He's all lined up.'

'Oh good. Who is it?'

'That'll be my secret.'

'*Oh*, Miss Bennett.'

'You'll find out, tomorrow night.'

'Is it someone I know?'

'That'd be telling.'

'You're awful!'

'An ogre.'

'Well, I'm just dying to see who it is. I'd better hang up, now. You must have a jillion things to do.'

'Nice talking to you.'

'Okay. Goodnight.'

'Night, Aleshia. See you tomorrow.'

She hung up, and stared across the kitchen at the pile

of Halloween themes. A *jillion things to do*. Seemed like a jillion, all right, when she had to struggle through pencil-written messes like that turkey Jim Miller turned in.

She took a sip of wine.

With a sigh, she returned to the table.

12

Just outside the city limits of Dendron, a town fifteen miles east of Ashburg, the Volvo slowed and swung into the driveway of the Sleepy Hollow Inn.

Sun eased off the gas. He watched Elmer drive up the L-shaped lane where half a dozen cars were already parked. The Volvo pulled into a space. Sam wanted to stop. He needed to see which room Elmer entered. The risk of being spotted was too great, though, so he drove past the motel.

He made a U-turn. He sped back to the entrance and pulled in, but Elmer was nowhere in sight. Slowly, Sam drove down the parking area. He counted twelve rooms, each with a bright orange door. Every room had two parking spaces. Elmer's Volvo was in front of Four, beside a white Datsun.

Probably, he'd gone into Four.

Light came through the room's pale curtains.

The spaces in front of Six were empty. Sam pulled in, and climbed from his car. A cold wind blew against him. He zipped his jacket, stuffed his hands into its pockets, and strolled up the walkway.

Slowing to listen at Four, he heard voices and laughter from a television. The sliding windows were shut. Nothing showed through the curtains. He kept walking.

He went to the motel office. It was well-lighted and warn. A young woman behind the registration desk looked up at him from a magazine. She took off her glasses and smiled. 'Hi. How are you tonight?'

'Just fine,' Sam said. Stepping close to the desk, he caught the odor of her perfume. The same perfume Cynthia wore. Suddenly, he was struck by her beauty: her wide eyes, her full lips and soft chin, the way her hair hung softly to her shoulders. She wore a white pullover that hugged her breasts.

'What can I do for you?' she asked.

Sam raised his eyes to her face. She looked amused, one eyebrow high. Was he *that* obvious about studying her? He blushed.

'I don't come with the rooms,' she said.

Sam laughed. 'You're a mind reader.'

'I know a randy man when I see one.'

'I'm randy, but I'm engaged.' It was a minor lie; he *felt* engaged, but so far hadn't asked Cynthia.

'Is the lucky girl with you?'

'Not tonight.'

'Then you'll probably want a single.'

He shook his head. 'I'm not here for a room.' Reaching into his rear pocket, he took out his billfold. He held it open on the desk. 'My name's Sam Wyatt.'

'Is that real gold?' the woman asked, staring at his shield.

'Gold-plated.'

'Okay if I touch?'

'Sure.'

Her fingertips stroked the badge. 'Say, that's nice.' She grinned up at him. 'Are you here to arrest someone?'

'Maybe.'

'Not me, I hope.'

'Not you.'

'That's good.' She slipped the badge out of the wallet. 'It's a heavy thing.'

'I need to know who's in number Four.'

'Sure.' She pinned the badge on her sweater. It dragged down the soft fabric, and settled on her left breast. 'How do I look?'

'Terrific.'

'Melodie Caine, homicide.' Folding her hands on the desk, she leaned forward. 'Are you a homicide cop?'

'Yeah,' he said, losing his smile. 'Afraid I am, tonight.'

Melodie's smile dissolved. 'I guess this is serious, then.'

'Yeah.'

'Hold on.' She opened a file box, flipped through a few cards, and pulled one out. 'This is the registration card for unit four.'

'Thanks.' Sam looked at the neatly printed name. 'Ms Mary Jones.' The home address was in Greendale, a suburb of Milwaukee.

'Is she your suspect?'

'Maybe.' Sam wished he'd thought to bring the photo along. 'What'd she look like?'

Melodie's heavy lips pressed together. Her eyebrows drew downward. 'She's about thirty-five or forty. She's a couple of inches taller than me, and thin. Too much make-up, especially around the eyes. I couldn't see what she was wearing, except for a gray trench-coat. I think she wore heels, though. And nylons, of course.'

'What color was her hair?'

'Blond. Dishwater blond.'

'When did she arrive?'

'Tonight. Half an hour ago, I guess. Think she's the one?'

'I don't know. Could be.'

'Want to find out?'

Sam nodded.

Melodie bent down, the badge swinging as it tugged her sweater out. She straightened, and dangled a key in front of Sam. 'Okay if I come along?'

'Better not. I don't expect trouble, but you never know.'

She gave him the key. 'Hurry back.'

Sam left the office. He was halfway to the room when he realized Melodie still had his badge. He didn't want to bother going back for it.

'Sam?'

He looked around. Melodie was standing in the office doorway, the wind blowing her hair.

'Want your badge?' she asked.

'Later.'

She stayed in the doorway, and folded her arms across her breasts. Sam turned away. He walked to the door of Four. Standing aside, he knocked. Seconds passed. He knocked again.

Over the sound of the television, a woman's voice called, 'Who is it?'

'Ms Jones?' he asked.

'Just a minute.'

He lowered his hand, and popped open the safety strap of his holster. His stomach felt tight. He took a deep breath, trembling as he exhaled.

The door opened several inches until its guard chain rattled taut. A woman's face appeared in the gap. Her eyes met Sam's. She blinked, and her mouth dropped open. 'Mr *Wyatt*?'

He stared, confused, trying to recall where he'd seen her. Then he remembered. This morning. Across the street from Dexter's house. 'Mrs Barnes?'

'What ... what are you doing here?'

'Is Elmer Cantwell inside?'

'No.'

'His car's parked in front.'

'So? I don't know any Elmer Cantwell.'

'Who's with you?'

'My husband.'

'You came all the way out here to a motel with your husband?'

'Yes. We ... like the privacy. Away from home.'

'I'd like to speak to him.'

'He's in the bathroom.'

'I can't leave until I've seen him.'

'Goddamn it,' she muttered. Tears glistened in her eyes.

'Mrs Barnes, I'm not interested in your personal life. I certainly have no intention of telling anyone you were out here. But I'm investigating a homicide, and I have to know if Elmer's in there with you.'

Holding her blouse shut with one hand, she wiped tears from her eyes and smeared her mascara.

'Tell him to come to the door.'

'He's not *here*.'

'Do you read the "Crime call" in the *Clarion*?'

Her chin started to tremble.

'If I have to arrest you, Mrs Barnes, you'll be reading about yourself. So will everyone else in town, including your husband and daughter.'

'You can't arrest me,' she muttered.

'Of course I can. Tell Elmer to come to the door. Right now.'

The door shut.

Looking to the side, Sam saw Melodie standing in the office doorway, still watching. She raised an open hand in greeting. Sam nodded.

He heard the guard chain rattle and skid. Then the door swung open. Elmer, fully dressed, smiled out at him. 'May I help you, *Mister* Wyatt?'

'I'm looking for Thelma.'

'Do you think she's here?'

'Mind if I look?'

Elmer blinked his bulging eyes. 'You've seen who's with me.'

'I'd like to look around.'

'You are a persistent devil.'

Elmer stepped aside, and Sam entered the room. The Barnes woman was nowhere in sight. One of the double beds was messed, its blankets still in place but rumpled. A bottle of Scotch stood on the night table, two drinking glasses beside it. Green slacks were folded neatly over the back of a chair.

Dropping to his knees, Sam glanced under the bed. Elmer chuckled.

Sam pulled open the closet door. Then he said, 'Ask Mrs Barnes to come out of the bathroom, please.'

'Do you really think that's necessary?'

'Yes.'

'Thelma is *not* hiding in the tub, if that's what's on your suspicious little mind.'

'I'd like to make sure.'

'With a loud sigh, Elmer stepped to the bathroom door.

'Ticia? *Mister* Wyatt wants you to come out.'

'No!'

'Do as he says, darling.' Elmer scowled at Sam. 'You've upset her terribly, you realize.'

The door opened. Ticia Barnes came out, her blouse now buttoned, a bathtowel wrapped around her waist. She glared at Sam. Her eyes looked red from crying, but the dark smudges of mascara were gone.

'Excuse me,' Sam said. He stepped past her, and entered the bathroom. He slid open the shower door. Nobody in the tub. He shut it. Turning away, he looked at the toilet. Its lid was down.

He glanced at the empty sink, then back to the toilet.

Crazy, he thought. But he couldn't stop himself.

Bending, he raised the lid.

A face looked up at him and he leaped back, gasping, before he realized he'd seen only his own reflection on the water. The lid crashed down.

'What *are* you doing?' Elmer asked.

Sam didn't answer. He stepped out of the bathroom.

'Did you find her?' Elmer asked, grinning. 'Was she hiding in the toidy?'

'Thanks for your cooperation,' Sam muttered. He walked toward the door.

Elmer stayed beside him. 'I am a trifle curious, *Mister* Wyatt. Did you follow me out here?'

'That's right.'

'You thought I'd lead you to Thelma? So sorry to disappoint you.' Elmer pulled open the door for him. 'Do have a pleasant evening.'

'If you know where Thelma is...'

'I haven't the vaguest. Nighty-night.'

Sam left. Walking toward Melodie, he heard the door shut.

'No luck?' she asked.

'A disaster.' He gave her the key, and followed her into the office.

'Let me get you some coffee. It'll make you feel better.'

'Sounds good,' he said.

'Come on through here.' Behind the registration desk, Melodie opened a door. 'Home sweet home.'

'This is where you live?' Sam asked. The softly-lighted room looked cozy.

'This is it. I've also got two bedrooms and a kitchen. Have a seat.'

He lowered himself onto the couch, and leaned back.

'Cream or sugar?'

'Just black.'

'Right.' She hurried across the room, her kilt flipping against her legs.

Sam shut his eyes. Let's not complicate the disaster, he warned himself, by getting involved with this gal. A cup of coffee, and that's it.

She came back with a ceramic mug in each hand. She gave one to Sam, and sat down beside him. He took a deep breath of her perfume.

'Must be a strange life,' he said.

'What?'

'Living in a motel.'

'I love it.'

'Meet lots of interesting people?'

She smirked. 'A few. You, for instance. You're very interesting.'

'I'm engaged, remember?'

'Engagements get broken.'

He looked at her hands. Both were wrapped around the mug, as if savoring its heat. She wore no ring on her left hand. 'You sound like you know.'

'First-hand.' She searched his eyes for a long time. 'You're not the kind of guy who dumps people,' she said, still staring.

'I try not to.'

'You've got such gentle eyes.'

'Well...' Blushing, Sam shrugged.

'Whoever you're engaged to, she's a lucky woman.'

'I keep telling her that.'

'She'd better know it.'

Sam took a sip of coffee. 'I have to get going.'

'Worried?'

'A little.'

'Don't be. I'm harmless.'

'Are you?'

'You're engaged, remember?' She sipped her coffee, and set the mug down on the table. 'I'd better give this back,' she said. Smiling, she lifted the badge. 'We're not pinned, after all.'

He watched her hands work at the clasp, and slide the badge off her sweater. It left two tiny holes over her breast.

She placed the shield on his palm, and folded his fingers over it. 'You're the first guy,' she said, 'who ever let me wear his badge.'

'Maybe we can do it again sometime.'

Her eyes turned sad. She gave his closed hand a quick squeeze. Then she let go, and stood up. She backed away, rubbing her hands on her kilt. 'Should I keep an eye on that room for you?'

'Not much point, I guess.' Sam finished his coffee, and stood. 'Of course, if another woman shows up ... I don't think that's likely to happen, though.'

He followed Melodie through the door to the office.

'I'll keep an eye out,' she said.

'I appreciate all your help. And your coffee.' Reaching for the doorknob, his back to Melodie, he felt uneasy – as if he'd forgotten something important. He turned to her, wondering what it could be. 'Thanks again,' he said.

'It's been nice knowing you, Sam Wyatt. However briefly.'

He pulled her against him, felt her softness and warmth, her lips and the wetness of her mouth. Then her cheek was damp against his face, and he saw that she was crying.

'I'm sorry,' he whispered.

She pressed her wet eyes to the side of his neck. 'That's okay,' she said. 'I was afraid you'd leave...'

'I have to.'

'...without kissing good-bye.'

13

Lynn Horner was watching television with her two boys when the lights went out.

'Oh no,' said the older boy, John.

'Hank?' Lynn asked. She saw the vague figure of her husband sit upright in his chair.

'Probably a fuse,' he grumbled. He sounded only half awake.

'Well, go see.'

'Yeah,' John said. 'We're gonna miss the best part.'

'That'd be a pity,' Hank said, getting to his feet.

'Just 'cause *you* fell asleep.'

'I'll go with,' said Mike.

'Sure, come on.'

The younger boy sprang to his feet. In the dark, he collided with his brother.

'Hey, watch who you're stepping on,' Joe complained. 'Klutz.'

'Oh, go soak your head.'

'*Boys*,' Lynn said.

Mike hurried after his father. 'Hey, wait up, Dad.'

'Get a move on, then,' his voice called from the hall. 'God forbid anyone should miss the end of the show.'

'Boy,' Joe muttered. 'What a crummy thing to happen.'

'It's not the end of the world,' Lynn said. Turning around on the couch, she pulled aside the curtain and looked outside. The nearby streetlight was shining brightly. There were no houses across the street, though, to check for lights. The trees on the golf course were blowing fiercely. 'The wind might've knocked down a power line,' she said.

'Wouldn't *that* be great.'

'You can always catch the rerun.'

'Sure. Six months from now. If we're home. If the television doesn't bust again.'

'You're probably just missing a commercial, anyway.'

'Yeah, sure.'

'I always thought it was fun to lose the power. It used to happen all the time, during thunderstorms. We'd get out candles, and tell scary stories...'

'Sounds like a ball.'

'My son, the cynic.'

'What's taking them so long?'

'Maybe a goblin got 'em.'

'Sure.'

'Ate 'em up.'

Joe laughed. 'You're nuts.'

'Ghoulies,' she moaned. 'And ghosties, and long-leggity beasties...'

'Oh, cut it out.'

'Tomorrow's Halloween. Maybe they're out early, this year, and came creeping and crawling out of their graves, looking for little boys.'

'*Mom.*'

'They get lonesome in their graves and crypts. On Halloween, they like to crawl out and creep around, and grab little boys to take back with them – to keep them company.'

'That's disgusting.'

'They like cynical little boys the best.'

'Yeah?'

''Cause they make such good conversation.'

'Sometimes I think you're cracked.'

'Woooooo.'

'Cut it out, would you?'

'*Woooooooo!*' Slowly, arms out, she stood up and stepped toward Joe. '*Woooooooooo*. Time to come with me to the grave. It's so cold and lonely down there.'

'Mom!'

She grinned at the tremor in his voice. 'And I get so *hungry*, down there.' She lunged at him.

Joe squealed and rolled out of her reach. 'Stop that!' he snapped, crawling across the carpet.

'You can't get away from me.' She lumbered toward him.

'Would you *stop*! I'm not amused.'

Lynn dropped her arms. 'Party pooper.' She returned to the couch, and flopped down. 'Must not've been a fuse,' she said. 'They'd have things fixed, by now.'

'Great.'

If the power isn't on by bedtime, she thought, she'd have to dig out the travel clock. Where had she stored it? She concentrated, and remembered leaving it in her suitcase so she wouldn't have trouble finding it, next time they took a trip. The suitcase was in the garage. Lovely.

'Jeez,' Joe said. 'The show's probably over, by now.'

'Well, those are the...'

The lights and television blinked on.

'There!'

'See what I told you?' Joe asked. The show's theme was playing as its credits rolled up the screen.

'Well, it's too bad. Could be worse, though.'

'I doubt it.'

'Why don't you go upstairs and get your p.j.'s on.'

'Mom!'

'It's nine o'clock.'

'It isn't fair.'

'You scoot upstairs and get ready for bed, then you can come down and watch TV until Mike's ready.'

'All *right*!' He scurried to his feet, and ran from the room. Lynn heard his footsteps pounding on the stairs.

The air in the den felt chilly. She pressed her legs together, and wrapped her red robe more tightly around herself.

Hank must've opened the back door, for some reason.

She folded her arms. Their warm pressure felt good on her taut nipples. She rubbed her legs against each other. Their skin was pebbled and achy with goose-bumps.

Had he *left* the door open?

She got up from the couch, and stepped out of the den. She walked down a dark hallway toward the kitchen. The swinging door was shut. A band of light showed beneath it.

Hank and Mike were sure taking their time. Maybe they'd decided to polish off the angel food cake.

Pushing open the door, she stepped into the kitchen.

Her bare foot splashed into blood. It slipped and shot forward. She fell back, grabbing the waste basket. It tumbled onto her, throwing coffee grounds and chicken bones on her robe. The door swung against her shoulder. Shoving it away, gasping, she sat up. The floor was puddled with blood, the oven door dripping.

'Hank!' she cried.

She struggled to her feet. She stepped past the refrigerator. Looking toward the alcove at the far end of the kitchen, she saw Hank sitting upright at the breakfast table. Mike lay on the table, shirt open, a knife and fork protruding from his belly.

'*Hank?*' she gasped.

She saw Hank's arm on the floor near his feet. Her mouth jerked open to scream. A hand covered it – a slippery hand that stank of blood. It yanked her backwards against a panting body. Another hand swung around from the side, plunging a carving fork toward her belly. She brought up her arms. The long tines jabbed into her forearm. Pain blasted through her.

Twisting, she kicked up her legs. The man lost his grip, and she fell to her rump. She flung herself sideways, rolling, and got to her hands and knees before the man grabbed the back of her robe collar and threw her down. Her back hit the floor.

He stomped on her belly, driving the wind from her. She doubled and clutched her knees until the man took her ankles. Her robe and nightgown flopped down, covering her face as he lifted her off the floor.

He swung her by the feet.

Swung her in a circle like a father playing with his child.

Faster and faster.

She tugged at the clothing bunched over her head. Pulled it free. Saw her naked body flying in circles around a huge, grinning man. One of her outflung arms struck the refrigerator. She had no breath to scream at the pain. The twirling man stepped closer to the refrigerator.

Next time around, more than her arm would hit.

She tried to curl forward but the momentum kept her stretched and the edge of the refrigerator door struck her face.

Joe Horner spat in the sink and rinsed his toothbrush. He cupped cold water with his hand, drank some, and rinsed the toothpaste foam off his lips and chin. Putting away his brush, he saw a glob of striped paste and streams of spittle in the sink. Mom, he knew, would nag if he left it there. But she wouldn't see it before Mike came in to brush his teeth. Let Mike take care of it. He dried his mouth and hurried downstairs.

Nobody in the den.

Great!

He flipped through the channels to *Night Beat*, a cop show he'd only seen once, on a fabulous night when Jean was babysitting and she let him and Mike stay up late if they promised not to tell.

He sat cross-legged on the floor.

Maybe, if he was really good, Mom and Dad would let him see the whole show. After all, he'd been cheated out of the last one.

Fat chance.

'Not on a school night,' they'd say.

Well, if they stayed away long enough...

He sighed with disappointment at the sound of footsteps in the hall.

'Hey, Dad, this is a really neat...'

The man who stepped into the den wasn't Dad.

14

Sam drove back toward Ashburg, listening to quiet music on the radio, his mind on Melodie and Cynthia and his new problem.

He wanted to see Melodie again. He wanted to look in her wide, eager eyes. He wanted to hear her voice. He wanted to hold her, and feel the warmth of her body against him.

Melodie, not Cynthia. Damn it, how could this happen? He'd thought he loved Cynthia, thought he wanted to marry her. It didn't seem right that suddenly, by accident, he should meet a woman who made him want to break away from her.

God, how could he do that to Cynthia?

'I'm not going to disappear,' he'd told her this morning.

'I've heard that before,' she'd answered.

Damn it, she *expected* him to dump her. As if she thought she deserved to fall in love with men and lose them. Life had taught her some nasty lessons: if Sam left her, he'd be adding his own.

He couldn't.

That's it for Melodie.

The pain of the thought made him want to jam on the

brakes, whip the car around and speed back to the motel. He would take Melodie in his arms, kiss ... *No!*

His clenched hands ached on the steering wheel.

I've chosen Cynthia, he told himself. I can't go back on her now. It's too late for that. In a few days, I'll forget all about Melodie.

No, I won't forget her.

But I can't have her. There's plenty of things you can't have, in this world, and you go along with it because you don't have a choice.

I have a choice here, though. I could stop seeing Cynthia, make up excuses...

That's no choice.

I just can't do that.

I can't.

Why, damn it to hell, did I have to follow Elmer out there tonight?

He pounded the steering wheel. He was tempted to bash his forehead against it, and wondered if he was going crazy.

Then, up ahead, he saw a quivering red glow in the sky.

'My God,' he muttered.

His foot rammed the gas pedal to the floor.

Must be the Sherwood place, he thought as he sped up the road. There were only a few houses this far out on Oakhurst, and the Sherwood house seemed most likely.

Not surprising for an abandoned structure like that to go up in smoke.

Kids or a derelict could've broken in, started a fire. Or Glendon Morley, its owner, might've finally decided to sell it to the insurance company.

Had to be arson. Had to be.

Swinging his car around a bend, Sam saw the last house on Oakhurst Road – the home of Clara Hayes. It was okay. Then the Sherwood place came into view, its front shimmering with fireglow, red emergency lights streaking across it. The next house was a pyre.

As he raced toward it, he tried to think who lived there. He didn't know. Parking in front, he leaped from his car. He spotted Berney near the tail of the hook-and-ladder truck parked in the yard, and ran to him.

'She's a goner,' Berney said.

'Whose place is it?'

'Horners.'

'They get out okay?'

Berney shook his head, his glasses flashing reflections of the blaze. 'Nobody's seen 'em,' he said. 'A neighbor down the road called in the alarm. By the time we got here...'

With a roar of crashing timber, a portion of the roof collapsed. Embers erupted into the red sky.

'Guess they cooked,' Berney said. 'Four of 'em. Two kids.'

'Maybe they weren't home.'

'Both cars in the garage.'

'Shit,' Sam muttered.

'Hasn't been a good day, not a good day at all.' Berney took off his glasses, and rubbed his eyes. 'You come up with anything on the Dexter business?'

'I'm still looking for Thelma.'

'Well, stick with it. She's as good a suspect as any, better than most.'

'Yeah.'

Berney held up his glasses. He squinted at the lenses, and blew on them. 'Damned ashes,' he said.

Sam turned away to watch the fire. The two white jets of water thundering into it seemed to have no effect. Eventually, though, the flood would knock the flames down.

Too late to save the house.

Much too late to save the family.

As he watched, another section of roof crashed down. The heat grew more intense on his face, and he turned away.

A small crowd was gathered beside the road, some folks chatting, most gazing up at the fire. He recognized a few of them: Basil White, Joan Trask, Cameron Watts. Was Clara Hayes among them? She'd been a good friend of Dexter, and Sam wondered if she'd heard about his death.

Everyone must know, by now.

As he looked for Clara, his eyes moved past the fire-red face of a teenaged boy. A familiar face. He went back to it, and his heart lurched.

Eric!

He shot a glance at every face near the boy, but didn't find Cynthia.

'See you later,' he told Berney.

'Right.'

The boy's eyes remained on the fire as Sam approached. He had the same, shiny eyes as his mother. The same delicate nose, and high cheekbones. Only the mouth looked alien to Sam – a long slit with almost no visible lips. Must be Scotty Harlan's mouth.

'Hi, Eric.'

The boy flinched. He looked at Sam, and took a step backwards, treading on a woman's foot.

'Ouch!' she cried.

Eric lurched away from her.

'Hell of a fire,' Sam told him.

Eric frowned, looking confused.

'Want a closer look?'

'The policeman told us to stay back.'

Sam gestured for Eric to come forward.

'You sure it's okay?'

'Sure.'

Eric stepped onto the lawn.

Turning away, Sam walked toward the hook-and-ladder. He stopped at its front. A moment later, Eric appeared beside him.

'The view's better from here.'

'Yeah,' Eric said, gaping at the blaze.

'I guess the people got killed.'

Eric wrinkled his nose. 'Yeah,' he said. 'Gross.'

'You didn't know them, did you?'

'I've seen 'em around. Joe, mostly. He was a jerk.'

'Not anymore.'

'Yeah.'

'Is your mother here?'

He shook his head, glanced at Sam, and quickly looked back to the fire.

'How'd you get here?'

'Walked.'

'Does your mother know?'

'She's not home. What're they gonna do with the bodies?'

'They'll bring 'em out, once the fire's cold. That won't be for a long time, though. How about a ride home?'

'No, that's okay.'

'Come on, Eric.'

He scowled up at Sam. 'I don't feel like it.'

'Why not?'

'Doesn't matter.'

'Are you mad because of last night?'

'Maybe.'

'Well, I can understand that. I'm sorry it happened, too. It was a hell of a way to meet. But can't we forget about that, and start over?'

'Why should we?'

'I'd like to be friends.'

'I don't need a friend like you.'

'Like me?'

'All you care about is messing around with Mom.'

'Eric, your mother and I . . .'

'Now you want to kiss up to me and get me on your side so you don't have to sneak around anymore behind my back. Well, screw you!'

'Eric!' Frowning, Sam reached for the boy's shoulder.

Eric knocked his hand aside, whirled around, and ran for the road. Sam decided to let him go. He wouldn't accomplish much by intimidating the kid. Better to work on him gradually, winning his trust a bit at a time.

He turned away. For a while, he watched the fire. Flames still reached out the windows. They burned inside the structure and clawed at the sky through the blazing skeleton of rafters.

Sam turned around, and scanned the crowd for Eric.

The boy was gone.

15

Eric ran past the last house on the road, and ducked behind a telephone pole. From there, he looked back at the distant group of people watching the fire. Nobody seemed to be coming, so he raced to the side of the house. Keeping close to the wall, he walked through the grass to the back yard. Light from a kitchen window lit the lawn below it.

The old woman, he thought, might be looking out. Could she see him if he crossed the dark part of the yard by the graveyard fence? Maybe. He might be safer, though, staying close to the wall and sneaking under the window.

Eyes on the back door, he rushed past the steps and crouched against the siding. Though the window was high enough to walk past, he dropped to the ground. The grass was cool and slippery on his hands. The dew quickly soaked through the knees of his jeans. As he crawled beneath the window, he held his breath.

She was at the window, glaring down – he knew she was. Any second, she would fling open the window and reach down for him, grab him by the neck, drag him into the house . . .

That's dumb, he told himself. She couldn't reach down this far, even if she tried.

As soon as he was past the window, he scurried to his feet and ran. He didn't stop until he reached the corner of the house. Looking back, he saw only the lighted window and the deserted yard. He leaned against the wall, breathing hard.

Stupid to be so scared of an old lady, he thought. He could always outrun her.

Easing away from the wall, he studied the area ahead. A flowerbed marked the edge of the old woman's property. He would have to jump that, then race across a wide space to the garage of the Sherwood house.

He looked around the corner, toward Oakhurst Road. Seeing no one, he stepped into the open. Headlights appeared. With a gasp, he leaped back and pressed himself to the back wall. He waited, then looked again. The car was gone. Nobody was in sight. He sprinted across the grass. Dead leaves crashed as his foot hit the flowerbed. He cringed at the noise, but kept running.

Still nobody by the road.

Still nobody behind him.

He dashed behind the garage. Safe there, he walked slowly through the weeds, catching his breath. He peered around the corner. The side of the house blocked his view of the road.

He'd made it!

With a sigh of relief, he walked from the garage to the back porch of the house. He silently climbed its steps. The screen door groaned as he pulled it open. No longer afraid of being heard, he grinned at the sound.

What a great place for a Halloween party!

The porch floor creaked under his sneakers. He twisted the doorknob, and pushed the door open. He stepped inside.

Nothing moved in the dark kitchen. He walked slowly through it, and pushed open the door to the dining room.

The room smelled strongly of paint.

He entered, and shut the door. His eyes searched darkness so intense that he blinked to be sure his eyes weren't shut.

'Hello?' he whispered.

He waited, listening. The silence was so complete that he heard quiet ringing inside his head – a high-pitched hum as if his brain were a television with its volume off.

'Hello?' he whispered again. 'It's me, Eric.'

When no response came, he walked through the darkness with his arms outstretched, seeking a wall. With each step, he half expected to bark his shin or stumble. What if the floor suddenly ended, and he lowered his foot into nothingness!

Don't be a dope, he told himself.

He'd been in here before. There was no furniture to trip over, no hole in the floor.

Feeling the black air, he continued walking slowly until his foot struck an object. He stumbled forward, stepping on something with his other foot, losing his balance completely and falling through the darkness. The floor came from nowhere, battering his hands and elbows and knees.

'What are you doing here?' The voice was a low whisper, scratchy and hardly audible. It came from the blackness ahead of Eric.

'I wanted to see you,' Eric said.

'I told you to stay away.'

'But the fire. The house next door. I was afraid you might want to call off the party.'

'It won't be called off. Did you make the invitations?' Eric nodded.

'Did you?'

'Yes.'

'You sent them to all your enemies, everyone who has ever punched you, or laughed at you, or spit in your face?'

'Well . . .'

'Answer me.'

'I mailed them to all the *kids*. What about grown-ups, though? There's a guy at school, Mr Doons. He's really mean to me. He made me do push-ups in piss. And Miss Major. I kind of got back at her, already, but she slapped me right in front of the whole class.'

'Slapped you? Why?'

'She said I was looking down the front of her dress.' Eric heard soft, hissing laughter. 'It was her fault, though. She kept bending over, and her dress was sort of loose, and she wasn't even wearing a bra.'

'Got a good look, did you?'

'Yeah, but she slapped me.'

'Go ahead and invite her.'

'What about Mr Doons?'

'Him too. Anybody you want, invite 'em. The more, the merrier.'

Eric grinned into the darkness. 'We'll really scare the hell out of them, won't we?'

'They'll never give you grief again.'

'I can't wait.'

'Won't be long, now.'

'Can you show me how you fixed the place up?'

'Not now.'

'Please?'

'Never beg, kid.'

Eric nodded, blushing. 'I won't again. I promise. Is it real scary, though?'

'Real scary.'

'Whatever I tripped on, was that part of the decorations?'

'Yeah.'

'Boy, this is gonna be the best Halloween party ever. Maybe we can do it every year. You know, make it an annual thing.'

'Sure.'

'You won't go away again, will you?'

'I'm here to stay.'

'Great! Hey, maybe you and Mom can get back together again. Wouldn't that be neat? You could get married, and...'

'She doesn't want me.'

'I bet she'd like you fine, once she got to know you.'

'No.'

'You could at least try, Dad. Ask her for a date, or something.'

'You better get out of here. Make sure nobody sees you leave.'

16

When Sam drove home, he saw Cynthia's car parked in front of his duplex. He pulled into the driveway, and hurried to his door. As he searched through his keys, the door swung open.

Cynthia smiled out at him. 'May I help?' she asked. She was wearing one of his big, flannel shirts. Her legs were bare.

Sam entered. He shut the door, and took her into his arms. 'That helps,' he said. 'A lot.' He pressed his mouth to her full, open lips. His hands moved down her back, stroked her buttocks through the soft flannel, slipped under the hanging shirt-tail and caressed her bare skin. He moved them upward, feeling the warm smoothness of her back. 'I thought we weren't going to see each other, tonight.'

'I thought so, too,' she said, pressing herself tightly against him.

'What happened?'

'I heard about Dexter on the news. I thought you might ... want some company.'

'Did you wait long?'

'I came over about nine.' She kissed the side of his neck. 'You smell like smoke.'

'I was at a fire.'

'A fire?' she asked, her lips tickling his neck.

He didn't want to tell her about the fire, just now. He didn't want to think about it, or about Eric or Dexter, about the Sleepy Hollow Inn where he nearly let himself abandon Cynthia for a smiling blonde with a badge on her breast. He wanted to forget it all, forget everything except the way she felt in his arms.

But he couldn't.

'A house burnt down, over on Oakhurst Road.'

She looked up at him, concern in her clear eyes. 'Whose house?'

'The Horners. Do you know them?'

'Lynn Horner? I met her at PTA.' She read the expression on Sam's face. 'Oh no.'

'I left before they went in for the bodies.'

'Did all of them . . .?'

'Apparently.'

'Oh geez.'

'I saw Eric at the fire.'

She stiffened. 'Eric? What was he doing there?'

'Watching. There were quite a few spectators.'

'He was supposed to be home.'

'I guess he heard the fire trucks, and got curious. Fires have a way of drawing people. He said you weren't home.'

'You talked to him?'

'For a couple of minutes. He didn't seem too happy about it. I offered him a lift home, but he ran off.'

Cynthia sighed and shut her eyes. 'Damn it, I shouldn't have left him. May I use your phone?'

'Sure.'

She looked up at him. With a half-smile, she drew her fingertips along his cheek. 'I just wanted to be with you,' she said. Then she turned away.

Sam watched her cross the room. She bent over the phone, and dialed. For a moment, Sam looked at the pale slopes of her exposed buttocks. The view started to arouse him, so he looked away. He wandered into the kitchen, and took a beer from the refrigerator. Snapping open the top, he returned to the living room.

Cynthia hung up. 'He didn't answer. I guess I'd better go back.' She smiled hopefully. 'Want to come?'

'If you want me to.'

'I want you to.'

Sam drank half his beer on the way back to the refrigerator. He put the can away, and returned to the living room. Cynthia wasn't there. She came in from his bedroom, a moment later, wearing shoes, tan corduroy pants, and a white bra. As she walked, she put on her blouse. Sam opened the door for her. 'I'm awfully sorry about this,' she said.

'Don't be.' He clutched the back of her neck. She smiled with disappointment, and stepped out the door.

They took separate cars to her house, several blocks away. Inside, Sam waited while Cynthia wandered through the house calling out for Eric.

She came back, shaking her head. 'He's not here, Sam.'

'Has he done this sort of thing before?'

'Sneaked out at night? No. Not that I know of. Damn it, I trusted him. We had a deal that we'd tell each other, whenever we went out. You know, so the other wouldn't worry and we'd know where to get in touch. He isn't supposed to go out, at all, when I'm gone at night.'

'I guess the temptation was too great, this time.'

'Yeah. Well, he was upset tonight. Maybe he did this to get even. Eric likes to get even. Of course, I guess he didn't know I'd find out.' She sighed. 'How about a drink? Let's have a drink, and give him a few minutes, and if he isn't here by the time we finish, we'll go out looking.'

'Fine with me.'

'A beer or a gimlet?'

'How about straight vodka with a slice of lime?'

'Aye-aye.'

They went together into the kitchen. Cynthia took glasses down from the cupboard, and Sam removed a quart of Gilby's from her cabinet.

'What upset Eric?' he asked.

'Well, we started off talking about you. Then it got around to his father. Eric seems to think I cheated him out of a dad by not marrying Scotty Harlan.'

'Does he know about Scotty?' Sam asked, surprised.

'You think I'd tell him that he's the product of a rape? He's got enough problems without having *that* laid on him. I just told him that we hardly knew each other, and got carried away one afternoon and that Scotty left town before he was born. Pretty much what I'd told him before. But he got all upset and kept saying I should've married the creep.'

'If he feels that way, maybe you should tell him the truth.'

'I can't.'

They finished making the drinks, and went into the living room. They sat on a couch.

'I think it'd help,' Sam said, 'if he got to know me.'

'You're probably right.'

'Why don't we plan something for Saturday? There's a football game at city college.'

'He isn't much for football.'

'What does he like?'

'Well, movies.'

'Okay. We'll go to the movies, then. He can pick what we see. We'll stop by the Pizza Palace, first, for supper.'

'All right.' She frowned into her drink, and took a sip. 'I just don't want him hurt again.'

'He won't be,' Sam told her. Suddenly, his heart began to race. 'Neither will you.'

She stared at him.

Sam's mouth went dry. He took a drink. His hand trembled as he lowered his glass to the table. He faced Cynthia. She kept staring. He saw fear and hope in her eyes as if she knew what was in his mind.

'How would you like to marry me?' Sam asked.

She raised a hand to her mouth. The fingertips pressed against her tight lips. 'Are you serious?' she asked through her fingers.

'I know this isn't a great time to ask. I'd planned to take you out for a fancy dinner...'

'You really want to marry me?'

'I've always wanted to, ever since we met.'

Her eyes sparkled with tears. 'It isn't ... just because of Eric?'

'It's because of you.'

'Jeezus.' Her long fingers wiped the tears from her cheeks.

'What do you say?'

She couldn't say anything. Nodding, she threw herself against Sam and hugged him. After a while, she drew back. Smiling, she hugged him again. 'Cynthia Wyatt,' she said.

'Sounds good.'

'Sounds wonderful. Oh, Sam.'

'Huh?'

'I wish we could be like this forever.'

'We'd get stiff necks.'

Laughing, she kissed him. The front door opened, and she pulled quickly away as Eric walked in. She frowned at the boy. 'Where have you been, young man?'

'Didn't *he* tell you?'

'You're not supposed to leave this house, when I'm gone.'

He shrugged. 'I wanted to see the fire.'

'That doesn't matter. A rule's a rule.'

'I'm sorry,' he said.

'Go on up to your room.'

He glared at Sam, and went up the stairs.

'I'd better have a talk with him,' she said.

'Maybe I should leave.'

'No. I won't be long. Why don't you fix yourself another drink? I'll be down in a few minutes.'

Eric was buttoning his pajamas when his mother knocked and opened the door. 'What do you want?' he said.

'I want to know what you think you're doing.'

'Going to bed.'

'Knock off the smart answers, all right?'

'I just wanted to see the fire.'

'How did you know there *was* a fire?'

'The trucks went by.'

'They wouldn't pass here, going to Oakhurst Road. They'd be going the other way.'

Eric scowled. 'I was taking a walk, and they went by.'

'So you were already outside?'

'Yeah.'

'Why did you leave the house?'

'I felt like it.'

'Where were you going?'

'Nowhere. I just felt like getting out.'

'You must've been going somewhere.'

'I wasn't. I just felt cooped up. It isn't fair. You can go out whenever you want, and I have to stay home.'

'I never just leave without telling you. Didn't occur to you that I might worry?'

'I didn't think you'd find out.'

'Well, I did.'

'Only 'cause I ran into that damned cop.'

'Eric!' she snapped.

'Well, it's true. If he hadn't told, you never would've found out.'

'You think that would make it all right?'

'What you don't know, won't hurt you.'

She gazed at him, looking stunned. 'You don't really believe that.'

'Sure.'

'You think it's okay to do something wrong, as long as you don't get caught?'

Eric nodded.

'You can't ... Where on earth did you *pick* that up?'

He grinned. 'From you.'

'I never...'

'The way you sneak around, sleeping with guys. It's okay, as long as little Eric doesn't find out. What he doesn't know, won't hurt him. Isn't that so?'

'No!'

'Oh yeah?'

'I have every right to see any man I want. For Godsake, I didn't go on a date for ten years after you were born, and you have the gall to criticize my morals! Goddamn it, Eric...'

'You should've married Dad.'

'Your father was despicable and he probably still is, if somebody hasn't killed him by now.'

'Go to hell.'

She slapped him.

Eric smiled.

She whirled away and left the room, slamming his door so hard its noise hurt his ears and nearly brought tears to his eyes.

Sam heard the sharp crash of the door, and grimaced.

What am I getting into? he thought.

He took a sip of icy vodka, wondering if he'd made a mistake. What if the kid doesn't straighten out?

Better have a long engagement. Very long. Make sure Eric isn't going to sour everything. If it looks bad, maybe everyone will be better off just forgetting it.

He expected Cynthia to come downstairs right away. He grew restless as the minutes passed. Maybe he should've gone home, after all. Too late for that. He couldn't leave without saying good-bye, and if Cynthia was so upset that she didn't want to face him...

At the sound of quiet footsteps on the stairway, Sam got to his feet.

Cynthia came down the stairs, one hand gliding along the banister. She wore a white nightgown that Sam had never seen before.

'You all right?' he asked.

'This is our night, Sam. I won't let Eric ruin it.'

The gown floated against her body, transparent as gauze, as she slowly walked toward Sam.

17

Eric lay in bed, wide awake. He heard his mother and Sam walk up the hallway, whisper words too quiet to understand. He shut his eyes as his door opened.

Soft footsteps crossed his room.

The side of his mattress sank. He smelled his mother's perfume, and her hand stroked his cheek.

'Honey?'

He moaned as if waking up. As the fingers caressed his forehead, he opened his eyes. 'Huh?' he said.

'I'm sorry we quarreled.'

'Me too.'

'I was just so worried when you weren't at home.'

'I'm sorry.'

'I love you so much.' She bent down, and kissed him. 'We'll try to do better, okay?'

'Okay.'

'Goodnight, honey.'

'Night.'

He watched her walk toward the open door. The light from the hallway passed through her nightgown, and made her look naked. He stared at her breasts as she turned to pull the door shut.

She's dressed like that for Sam, he thought.

The dirty bastard.

He's probably waiting in her room, right now, taking off his clothes.

If Dad only knew ... *He's* the one who should be going to bed with her, not this damned cop.

Eric climbed from bed. He found his sneakers, and went to his door. He listened for a moment. Hearing nothing, he opened his door and looked out. The hallway was dark. It looked deserted.

He stepped out, and silently closed his door. He tiptoed along the hall to the head of the stairway. The house below him was dark. A few of the stairs creaked as he descended, but nobody came to check.

He hurried into the kitchen, and turned on the light. A paring knife lay on the counter beside a carved lime.

It might break, he decided.

So he slid a butcher knife out of its rack. Holding it behind his back, he rushed to the front door. There, he put on his sneakers.

He ran across the yard, gritting his teeth against the chilly wind that blew through his pajamas. As he ran, he glanced up at the windows of his mother's room. They were dark. Crouching by the front of Sam's car, he stabbed the side of the tire. The point didn't penetrate enough. He worked the knife with both hands, pushing hard against it. Suddenly, it rammed deep. Rubber-smelling air hissed into his face.

As the corner of the car sank, he crawled to the rear. He sat on the wet grass, feet against the tire. Leaning forward, be held the knife to the whitewall. He stomped his heel against its butt. The knife punched in.

Eric tugged the knife free, and stepped into the street.

He sat down on the cold pavement, held the knife in place, and kicked. It went easily into the third tire.

He did the same to the final tire.

That'll fix you, he thought.

His jaw hurt from clenching his teeth. He opened his mouth wide, and tried to work out the tension.

Peeling the wet pajamas away from his rump, he looked up and down the block. He saw no one. He glanced again at his mother's windows.

They're too busy to see me, he thought.

It didn't matter, though.

Sam would know who'd done it.

Maybe the dirty bastard would get the message.

Eric ran back to the house. He entered its warmth, and took off his shoes. Picking them up, he walked silently into the lighted kitchen.

The knife blade was streaked with black from the tires.

If he put it back in the rack without cleaning it ... How could he clean it without making noise? Soap and water might not work, anyway. He'd need to use paint thinner, or nail polish remover, something like that. Rubbing alcohol? A whole bottle of it stood in the medicine cabinet.

Turning off the light, he left the kitchen. He held the knife behind his back, and went to the stairway. The hall above was still dark. He slowly climbed the stairs, cringing each time the wood creaked under his feet.

At the top, he looked down the hall. The door of his mother's room was still shut. He turned to the right, and tiptoed into the bathroom.

He locked the door. He flicked the light on, and

opened the medicine cabinet. The rubbing alcohol sloshed in its plastic bottle as he lifted it down. He poured the clear liquid onto a wad of toilet paper. It soaked through, feeling strange on his fingers – burning and cool at the same time.

He rubbed it on the knife. The black streaks of rubber seemed to dissolve. In less than a minute the blade was sleek and shiny. He wiped it dry with more toilet paper, tossed both wads into the bowl and automatically reached out to flush. As his fingertips touched the handle, he realized what he was about to do. He pulled his hand away.

With the bottle back in the medicine cabinet, he picked up his shoes and knife. He silently opened the door, and walked up the hallway. He passed the stairs. He continued up the hall and put his shoes just inside his room. As he pulled the door shut, he heard a quiet gasp.

It came from his mother's room.

Heart suddenly hammering, he tiptoed to her door. He stood there, listening. From inside came muffled sounds of harsh breathing and moans and the squeaking bed.

He saw that the door was open a crack.

His heart pounded so hard that he felt dizzy and sick.

Stepping forward, he pressed gently against the door. The crack widened.

In the light from the windows, he saw them. Their tangled, thrusting bodies were dark against the sheets. He couldn't tell one from the other.

Pushing the door wide open, he stepped into the room. He walked toward the bed.

It was Sam on top, Mom under him with her knees up, hands clutching his back as his ass jerked up and down. She writhed, gasping and moaning.

Eric stopped at the foot of the bed. He gripped the knife so tightly that his hand ached.

Such awful sounds. Flesh pounding flesh. Wet, sticky noises. Grunts like wallowing pigs.

'Bastard,' he muttered.

'Eric?' gasped his mother. 'Oh my God!' Her hands pushed at Sam but he clung to her. 'No!' she cried.

Sam's body stiffened and jerked.

He quickly rolled off.

Mom squirmed over the sheet. Reaching down beside the bed, she picked up her nightgown. She pressed it to her body, sat up, and turned on the bedside lamp.

'*Eric!* Put down that knife!'

'He's not my dad,' Eric said.

'Put down that knife!'

He slashed the palm of his left hand. Blood spilled from the slit.

Mom screamed.

Sam lunged off the bed at him, smashing the knife from his hand and throwing him backward to the floor.

18

They spent nearly two hours at Emergency, most of it waiting because an eighteen-wheeler rear-ended a passenger car out on the highway. Eric sat beside Cynthia, mute and staring.

When they finally got back to the house and put him to bed, Cynthia suggested that Sam go home.

'Eric's so upset,' she said. 'Maybe ... I don't know ... Maybe you'd better not stay tonight.'

'He's asleep now.'

'Maybe he is and maybe he isn't.'

'If you want me to leave, I will. But I don't think it'd be smart to reward Eric, that way. You'd be letting him win, teaching him that it works to bust in on people, mutilate himself, slash tires...'

'I guess you're right,' she admitted.

They went to bed, then. For a long time, Sam couldn't sleep. He lay beside Cynthia, staring into the darkness, knowing that she was also awake. They didn't talk or touch. When Sam finally fell asleep, he dreamed he was awake.

He dreamed that Eric stood at the foot of the bed, knife ready. He was safe as long as Eric thought he was sleeping. But a heavy, bloated spider was scurrying down the wall. In seconds, it would creep onto Sam's face. He wondered, vaguely, how he could see the spider so well with his eyes shut.

They're open!

With a sudden grin, Eric dived onto him. The blade plunged into his stomach, stiff and cold.

He sat up, grabbing his stomach, gasping.

For a long time after that, he lay awake. He didn't want to fall asleep if it meant returning to the dream. So he kept his eyes open, and tried to think of something pleasant.

His thoughts drifted to Melodie Caine.

They were in the motel office, and she wore her white sweater and kilts. Sam shut his eyes to see her more clearly.

'If I'm supposed to be your deputy,' she said, 'I need a badge.'

He held it out to her.

'No, you have to pin it on me or it's not official.'

He tried to pin the badge to her sweater, his fingers trembling against her breast.

'Don't be nervous,' she whispered. She jumped and said 'Ouch!' as he stuck her.

'Are you okay?'

'I don't know.' She lifted her sweater over her full, milk-white breasts. A spot of blood shimmered above the nipple. 'You'd better kiss it and make it well.'

He pressed his lips to the wound, tasting the warm salty blood. Then her nipple was in his mouth. His teeth teased the springy column of flesh; his tongue flicked and circled.

'Oh Sam,' she gasped. 'Oh Sam, I love you.'

19

Half an hour before classes began, the first floor hallway of the main building was nearly deserted. Eric stopped in front of the door marked MR DOONS, VICE PRINCIPAL. He glanced both ways. Nobody was nearby or watching. He crouched, slid an envelope under the door, and walked away.

Upstairs, he passed a couple of girls standing at an open locker. They paid him no attention. He walked by an open classroom.

What if Miss Major's door was open?

As he approached it, his heart started to pound, sending throbs of pain into his wounded hand.

Her door was shut.

He glanced back at the girls. Their backs were turned. He flipped open the cover of his English grammar text, and took out an envelope. Crouching, he dropped the envelope to the floor and pushed it toward the slot beneath the door.

The door sprang open.

Eric jumped back.

Miss Major looked down at the envelope, then at Eric. She planted her fists against her hips, and Eric realized she was wearing the same dress she'd worn the day he saw her breasts, the day she slapped him.

Her toe nudged the envelope. 'I assume it's for me,' she said.

Eric nodded.

Miss Major held out her hand. Her long fingers trembled slightly, and Eric wondered if she was afraid of him. Probably not. She looked angry, not frightened. 'Give it to me.'

He picked up the envelope, and laid it across her hand.

She turned it over. She ran it through her fingers. Her eyes fixed on Eric. 'I'll give you one chance. You can take it back now, unopened, and that'll be the end of it.' She held it toward him.

Eric's hand throbbed. The pain made it hard to think. He wanted to accept the envelope and get far away from Miss Major. But he didn't want to back down.

'What'll it be, Eric?'

'I guess I'll take it,' he mumbled, and reached for the envelope. As his fingers closed on it, she snatched it away. Her tight mouth smiled.

'You said...'

'I changed my mind. I just can't wait to see what it is that you're so eager to take back, now that you're caught.'

'It's nothing.'

'I'll just bet.' She slipped a finger under the flap, and slowly worked it up the envelope, ripping the seam. 'Well well well, what have we here? Not another rat, obviously.' She plucked out the paper and unfolded it. 'Join the fun,' she read in a mocking voice. With a frown, she read the rest in silence. She gazed at the paper for a long time, as if reluctant to meet Eric's eyes. Her face was red. Finally, she lowered the invitation. 'You're giving a party?' she asked.

Eric nodded. He smiled, trying to look embarrassed. 'I thought you might like to come, if you're not too busy. It'll be a bunch of kids and a few of my teachers and Mr Doons.'

'But why me?'

'Well.' He shrugged. 'I feel bad about – you know – what happened. I just thought maybe you could come and have a good time, and maybe we wouldn't have to be enemies anymore.'

'That's very thoughtful of you, Eric.' She looked again at the invitation. 'You're having it at the Sherwood house?'

'Yeah. We've got it all fixed up for the party. It'll be real spooky.'

'But it's abandoned, isn't it?'

'Oh, my mom's good friends with the owner.'

'Glendon Morley?'

'Yeah. He's gonna be there, too. So's my mom and some of her friends.'

'Sounds like you'll have quite a crowd.'

'Yeah. I hope you'll come. You can bring along a friend, too, if you want.'

She folded the invitation and slipped it into the envelope. 'We'll see,' she said. 'I'll try to make it, if I can. At any rate, I appreciate being invited.'

Eric smiled and shrugged.

With a friendly nod, she stepped into her classroom and shut the door.

Eric started down the hall. At first, he felt only relief at escaping her wrath. Then he thought of her embarrassment, and smiled.

He had really put one over on her. All his lies had worked. Moreover, she'd sounded as if she might actually come to the party. In triumph, he slapped his leg – and yelped as pain streaked up his arm.

20

'Are you all right?' Betty asked when he entered the station the next morning.

'Hanging in there,' Sam said, and yawned. He poured himself a mug of coffee. 'Cynthia's son cut himself, last night, and we took him over to Emergency.'

Betty frowned. 'I hope it wasn't too serious.'

'Took a dozen stitches,' he said. He sipped the coffee, and sat at his desk. 'How are *you* doing?'

'Managing,' she said. 'It isn't going to be quite the same around here without Dexter. He was...' She pressed her lips tightly together. Her chin trembled. She reached for a tissue and covered her eyes. Sam looked down.

He took small drinks of coffee, the steam burning his raw eyes.

God what a night, he thought.

Betty blew her nose. 'Anyway,' she said, 'I heard you were out at the fire.'

'Yeah.'

'They couldn't find the Horners.'

'*What?*'

'Apparently, everyone thought they were burnt. But the fire department searched through the rubble and couldn't find their bodies. So it looks as if they weren't home last night, after all.'

'Well, that's lucky. Where were they?'

Betty shrugged. 'Nobody knows. They haven't shown up. Chet's supposed to check the bus terminal and taxis.'

'Berney thinks they skipped?'

'He does. Hank Horner is now topping his suspect list.'

'He thinks Horner killed Dex?'

'Killed him, panicked, and sneaked out of town, last night, with his family.'

'Why would he burn the house?'

'So we'll assume he's dead.'

'We're not going to assume he's dead if we don't find the body.'

'Oh, you know *people*.' She made a weary smile. 'Horner probably didn't know any better. He figured, if he burnt the house down, we'd think he and his family got turned to ashes.'

'Not a very smart fellow.'

'Murderers aren't normally famous for their brains.'

'Has Berney come up with a motive?'

'Not yet. He's going over to Horner's office, this morning. You're supposed to continue with the Thelma angle. Oh, a call came in for you, a few minutes ago.' She glanced down at the log book. 'A Miss Melodie Caine.'

The name slammed into him. His heart raced and his mouth went dry.

'You're supposed to call her right away.'

He swallowed. 'Did she leave a number?'

Betty read the number, and Sam copied it with a shaky hand.

He dialed from the phone at his desk. As he listened to the ringing, he nearly hung up; he could drive out to the motel, and get her message in person. The idea excited him, but he'd promised himself to stay away. He would hold to that promise.

I'm committed to Cynthia now, he thought.

For better or worse.

'Sleepy Hollow Inn,' said the low, familiar voice.

'Melodie, this is Sam Wyatt.'

'Good. I'm glad you got back to me so fast. I've got something for you, Sam. You know those people in room Four? Well, one of them – the man – made a telephone call after you left. He called from his room, so I had to put it through for him. Would you like to know the number?'

'I sure would.'

'Thought you might.'

Sam copied the number as she gave it to him. 'That's great, Melodie. Thanks a lot.'

'Hey, let me know how it all turns out, okay?'

'I will.'

'Take care, Sam.'

'You too.'

Her telephone clacked down. For a moment, Sam listened to the empty, desolate sound of the empty wires. Then he hung up.

'Got something?' Betty asked.

'Could be.' He flipped through the special directory listing its entries by telephone number.

* * *

A woman in jeans and a sweatshirt opened the door. Sam gazed at her dishwater blond hair, her haggard, familiar face. 'Thelma?' he asked.

'I'm Marjorie,' she said.

Sam glanced at his note pad. 'Are you Mrs Doons?'

'That's right.'

'You look ...'

'Thelma's my sister.'

'Twins?'

'We're a couple of years apart. If you're looking for Thelma, she's not in.'

'Is she staying with you?'

The woman nodded.

'Could I talk to you?'

'Come in.'

He followed her into the living room, and took a seat. 'I'm Sam Wyatt,' he said.

'You're here about Dexter.'

'Yes.'

'God, that was a terrible thing.'

'Where is Thelma?'

'She's spending the day in Dendron with our mother.'

Dendron again. As if fate were trying to drag Sam back there, back to the Sleepy Hollow Inn and Melodie. 'Your mother lives in Dendron? Could I have her address?'

'There's really no point in that. Thelma'll be home this evening. Why don't I have her phone you when she arrives?'

'I'd prefer to see her as soon as possible.'

Marjorie sighed. 'If you insist, then. It's 354 Tenth Street.'

'Thank you,' he said, writing it down. 'When did Thelma arrive in town?'

'Tuesday morning.'

'And she's been staying here with you?'

Marjorie nodded. 'If you think she had anything to do with Dexter's death, you're wrong. It's just an unfortunate coincidence that she happened to be in town, this week. She's been back – oh, two or three times a year since she and Dexter split up. Nothing ever happened before. If she wanted to kill him, she had plenty of chances to do it before now. She was finished with Dexter the night she walked out on him.'

'Why did she come to town this week?'

'Tomorrow's my birthday.'

'She came in from Milwaukee to celebrate your birthday?'

'Oh, she hasn't lived in Milwaukee for years. She went there with Babe Rawls. They were only together for six months or so. He treated her shamefully – beat her up all the time and subjected her to ... well, I needn't dwell on all the sordid details. Suffice it to say that she had enough of it, and left him. She's been living in Hayward for the better part of a year.'

'Do you know where she was Wednesday night?'

'She spent the night here.'

'Did she go out?'

'Why, yes. She went over to the Sunset Lounge.'

The Sunset Lounge. Sam had been there himself that night, with Cynthia. Of course, he hadn't been looking for Thelma then. At that point, he hadn't even known what she looked like. She might have been sitting at the next table.

'Did she go there alone?'

Marjorie shook her head. 'She went with Ticia Barnes.'

Sam raised his eyebrows.

'They're old friends,' Marjorie explained. 'Ticia used to live next door to us, when we lived on Seventh Street.'

'What time did Thelma leave for the lounge?'

'Oh, nine-ish. You can check with Ticia, if you wish. She picked Thelma up.'

'What time did Thelma get back?'

'I have no idea.'

'You said she spent the night here.'

'And so she did. Phillip and I hardly felt it necessary to wait up for her. We went to bed at our usual time. Maybe Phillip heard her come in, but I'm afraid I was dead to the world. I haven't the vaguest notion what time she came in. I know she was here, though. She joined us for breakfast in the morning.'

'What time was that?'

'Seven.'

'And she didn't tell you what time she got home?'

'Not a word.'

'Did she say anything about what she'd done?'

'Oh, just that she and Ticia had a great time.'

'Did she say she'd met anyone?'

'No. But why don't you have a word with Ticia? I'm sure she can fill you in.'

21

At the ten-thirty 'nutrition break', Eric headed for the school library. With all the kids running loose, it was the only place of safety. He'd discovered this sanctuary during the second week of school, after spending his nutrition and lunch periods in terror.

Nate Houlder had chased him, that day, threatening to beat the shit out of him.

Eric barely made it to the library door. He rushed inside, Nate hot on his tail.

'Hold it!' Mr Carlson had yelled, his voice booming through the quiet library.

Eric stopped, but Nate kept coming and grabbed his arm.

'Let go of him!'

Nate dragged him toward the door.

Mr Carlson's face turned bright red and he suddenly ran from behind the circulation desk, his corduroy jacket fluttering behind him.

Nate hesitated, then smirked as if he thought the librarian was a joke. He pulled Eric toward the door.

'Damn it, you little...!' Carlson's hand chopped Nate's forearm. Eric pulled away from the loose fingers.

'You *hit* me,' Nate snarled.

'I told you to let go of him.'

'Man, I'm gonna sue your ass.'

'Be my guest. In the meantime, get out of here.'

Nate glared at him.

Carlson shoved him.

'Hey, don't push me!'

'Get out of here.'

Nate turned away. 'I'm going, I'm going.'

'Not fast enough.' Following the boy, Carlson nudged his trailing foot sideways and tripped him. Nate caught himself on the bar of the door. As he left, he looked over his shoulder. 'Goddamn fag. You two deserve each other.'

Eric smiled, remembering the scene. By driving him into the library that day, Nate had done him a real favor. His life at Ashburg High had improved a lot since discovering the refuge: nutrition and lunch periods were no longer times of being chased, punched, and trash-canned. Instead, he could sit in the safety of the library, read, or join the others chatting with Mr Carlson.

Of course, it was still a problem getting there unscathed. As he walked past the other students, today, he kept a sharp eye out for Nate and Bill and half a dozen other guys with nothing better to do than torment him.

Glimpsing someone close to his side, he took a quick step away and looked around. Only Beth. She smiled slightly, her lips together in a way she'd started smiling since she got her braces.

'What happened to your hand?' she asked.

'Ah, nothing. I cut it on a broken glass, last night.'

'Where're you going?'

'The library.'

'Me, too. No more snack bar for me.'

'You're not fat.'

She laughed softly. For a moment, her bright clear eyes met Eric's. Then she lowered them as if embarrassed. 'I'm not skinny, either.'

'Who says you have to be?'

'Oh, nearly everyone.'

'What do they know,' he said.

As they talked together, he sneaked glances at Beth. She was no taller than him, with light brown hair and a band of freckles across her nose and cheeks. He'd known her since she moved to Ashburg three years ago. She never made fun of his size or his mind, and she wasn't pretty enough to frighten him so they got along just fine.

'Are you going to the Halloween party?' Eric asked.

'Which one?'

'Which one?' He looked at her, frowning. 'The one at the old Sherwood house.'

'Do you think that's for real?'

'Sure. I got an invitation.'

'So did I, but I can't imagine the place will be opened for a party. It's been boarded up for years.'

'It'll be open tonight.'

'You sound awfully sure.'

'It just doesn't make sense for somebody to send out all those invitations and then not have a party.'

'I think it's just a gag,' Beth said.

Eric shook his head. 'Gee, I was hoping...'

'What?' She looked at him, smiling.

133

'I was kind of hoping you'd be there.' He reached for the library door.

'Wait. Let's not go in yet.'

Their eyes locked. He saw her blush, and felt heat rushing to his own face.

'Aleshia's having a party tonight.'

'She *is*?' Eric tried to keep his disappointment from showing. If Aleshia had a party, she wouldn't be at the Sherwood house. Not Beth, not Aleshia. How many others wouldn't show up? Maybe he'd be the only one . . .

'Eric, would you like to go with me to Aleshia's party?'

'Me?' He pictured Aleshia, lithe and smiling. At her party, he could look at her for hours, talk to her, maybe even somehow touch her, feel the warm smoothness of her skin. 'I'd sure like to . . .'

Beth shrugged. 'I know it's awfully late to be asking. You probably have other plans.'

'Sort of.'

'It's all right. I can ask somebody else.'

'No, don't. I'll go with you.'

'Really, you don't have to.'

'I want to. It's just that . . . I've got a problem about . . .' He sighed. 'I want to go to the Sherwood house.'

'What on earth *for*?'

'I guess because it's been shut up, all these years. I've always wondered what it must be like inside. Haven't you?'

'A little, maybe.'

'And it just seems like such a great place for a Halloween party.'

'Great, like a boneyard.'

'Yeah, that's just the point. And another thing is,

nobody knows who's giving the party. Like it's a big mystery. I'd like to go and find out.'

'I don't know.' Beth shook her head. 'I promised Aleshia I'd go to her party. I guess, if you really have to go to the other one ... Well, maybe I'd better find someone else for tonight.'

'Oh, don't do that.'

'What about the Sherwood house?'

'It won't be much fun, anyway, if nobody else is there.'

Beth smiled, this time not holding back to hide her braces, this time beaming.

22

'What do *you* want?'

'I'm sorry to bother you again, Mrs Barnes...'

'Then don't. I'm quite busy. My daughter is having a party tonight, and I've got a jillion things to do.'

'I won't take up much of your time.'

She looked past him as if she half expected neighbors to be gathering in the street. 'You'd better come in,' she said.

Sam followed her across the foyer. In the living room, Ticia stepped over a vacuum cleaner and sat on the couch. She folded her hands in the lap of her Sassoon jeans.

'If it's about last night,' she said, 'I frankly don't see why my private life is any of your business.'

'It's not about that. Where were you Wednesday night?'

Her pale skin turned red. 'What are you implying?'

'You weren't home Wednesday night. I'd like to know where you were.'

'I fail to see what this has to do with anything.'

'It has to do with Chief Boyanski's murder. Now, please answer the question.'

She stared at her folded hands, her eyes blinking

rapidly. 'All right,' she finally said. 'I have nothing to be ashamed of. I went to the Sunset Lounge.'

'Alone?'

Her eyes narrowed. 'You already know, don't you? Otherwise, you wouldn't be asking these questions.'

'I don't know as much as I'd like.'

'I went with Thelma. I picked her up at her sister's house.'

'What time?'

'Around nine.'

'When did you leave the lounge?'

'Midnight.'

'Did Thelma leave with you?'

She stared down at her hands. 'I really fail to see ...'

'She didn't leave with you?'

'We met some friends. After a few drinks, we went our separate ways.'

'When did Thelma and her friend leave?'

'They left a little earlier. Eleven-thirty, maybe.'

'Who did she go with?'

'You don't know?'

'I'm asking you.'

Ticia smiled. 'I do hate to disappoint you, but I don't know the man's name.'

'You and Thelma sat and had drinks with him for – what, two hours? – and you didn't catch his name?'

'He was at the bar. Thelma went to join him, while I stayed at the table with Elmer.'

'You were with Elmer Cantwell?'

'He doesn't know the man, either. We both thought it a trifle foolhardy of Thelma to go off with a stranger. Elmer was somewhat disappointed, too. I'm sure he'd joined us with the expectation of swooping away with Thelma. He hardly knew me, at that point.' Ticia smiled with satisfaction. 'I must say, however, his disappointment was short-lived.'

'You didn't see Thelma, after she left with the stranger?'

'Should we have?'

'Did you?'

'No, we saw neither hide nor hair of them, after that.'

'Have you seen Thelma, since then?'

'She phoned the next morning to say she'd had a wonderful time.'

'Did she mention what they did?'

Ticia grinned. '*Really*, Mr Wyatt. I think we can make certain assumptions on that score – no pun intended.'

Sam wasn't amused. 'Did she say where they went?'

'Somewhere private, I should imagine.'

'But she didn't say?'

'No, she didn't say. I think you'll have to ask Thelma about that.'

23

'Eric Prince?' Aleshia, walking with Beth during lunch period, rolled her eyes. 'He's such a simp. You certainly could've done better than Eric *Prince*.'

'I like him.' Beth dodged to safety as a boy raced by on the asphalt.

'I like Hostess Twinkies, for heaven's sake. That doesn't mean I have to *date* one.'

Beth shrugged and took a bite of her turkey sandwich. Mom had made it for her and used such a tiny speck of mayonnaise that the sandwich was too dry to eat. She managed to swallow the lump already in her mouth. 'There's nothing wrong with Eric,' she said.

'There's nothing wrong with Twinkies.'

'The guys just pick on him because he's smaller than they are.'

'If you prefer to think that, be my guest.'

'He's *not* a fag.'

Aleshia smiled. 'Is that a fact?'

'Everybody's a "fag" around here if he gets good grades and doesn't go out for football.' She tossed her uneaten sandwich. It vanished into a trash can, and thunked. 'Eric's just more sensitive than most of the other guys.'

'You must admit he's a trifle effeminate.'

'A little, maybe. Doesn't bother me. I mean, the guy hasn't got a father.'

'I always knew he was hatched.'

'I'm being serious. How can you expect a guy to act all tough and masculine when he's never had a father around to learn from?'

'Beats me. What're you going as?'

'We haven't decided. We're meeting after cheerleaders and going over some ideas. Do you know what you'll be wearing?'

Aleshia struck a pose, chin high, one eyebrow raised, fingers deep in her hair. 'Perhaps I'll come as myself, Aleshia, the divine one whose body lights men afire with pagan lust.'

'Lots of luck,' Beth said, and danced out of the way laughing as Aleshia kicked. Her shoulder struck someone. Her feet tangled. Hands flew and clutched her, pulling her down backwards. She landed on top of a sprawling boy.

'Hey, offa the merchandise,' he said.

Beth recognized the voice. Squirming onto her side, she saw the grinning, whiskered face of Nate Houlder.

'I mean, I know you're crazy about me but this is ridic...'

Her elbow dug into his ribs as she raised herself.

'Oomph! Jesus *Christ!*' He slammed her elbow away and she flopped onto him, her cheek against his scratchy chin, her breasts mashed against his chest, her hips inside his open legs.

Beth tried to push away, but he held her to him.

'Let go!'

'Nate Houlder!' Aleshia snapped.

Others had already gathered around, laughing and whistling and offering comments.

'Put it to her, Houlder!'

'Right on, right on!'

'Let her go!'

'Oaf.'

He bumped up against her, ramming his groin against her lap, bouncing her.

'Stop!' she cried.

'Have at it, Houlder!'

'Leave her *alone.*'

'Give her one for me!'

'Oooh baby,' Nate said. 'Oooh baby, I like it, I like it.'

'Teacher's coming!'

Nate suddenly flung her aside. She hit the asphalt, rolling against several feet as the crowd backed off. Through teary eyes, she saw Nate smash aside the spectators and disappear.

Aleshia and Mary Lou helped her up.

'All right!' shouted Mr Doons as he shoved through the ring of students. 'All right, break it up. What's going on here!' He clutched Beth's arm. 'What's going on?'

'Nothing,' she said.

'Yeah? How come you're crying?'

'Nate Houlder,' Aleshia said.

'He pushed her down,' said Mary Lou.

'No,' said a boy. '*She* pushed *him.* I saw it.'

'They were wrestling,' said a small girl in glasses.

'Okay, young lady, you come with me.' He pulled Beth by the arm.

'I didn't *do* anything.'

'Come along.' He pulled her through the crowd and led her across the asphalt yard.

Beth fought back her tears. Everyone was looking.

'Please,' she said.

'We'll discuss it in my office.'

There was a cold lump in her stomach. This can't be happening, she thought. She'd never been taken to the office before. She felt helpless and terrified.

They walked past one of the teachers, Mr Jones. He glanced at her, looking perplexed.

'You don't have to drag me,' she said to Doons.

He ignored her.

'I'm not a criminal.'

He pulled her up the back stairs and into the building. The hallway, at least, was deserted; students weren't allowed to wander inside during the lunch period. Halfway down the long hall, he opened a door. The paint on its frosted glass read MR DOONS, VICE PRINCIPAL.

'Inside,' he said, and let go of her arm.

She stepped into a carpeted room with a dozen empty chairs against its walls. Mrs Houston, a silver-haired secretary, looked up from her typewriter.

'Sit,' Mr Doons said. 'I'll see *you* later.'

Beth sat down, and Doons left.

Mrs Houston returned to her typing.

'Yeah, just like I was humping her. Should've been there, Bill-boy. The little twat didn't know whether to shit or go blind.'

Bill was glad he'd missed it. He'd been in classes with

Beth, here and in junior high, and he didn't like the idea of Nate bullying her. She was a soft-spoken, cheerful girl. If Nate wanted to dump on someone, he should've picked one of the bitches. Plenty of them around.

'Why *her*?' Bill asked.

'Like I said, man, she bumped into me.' He grinned. 'She's what y'call your "target of opportunity". I mean, you can't just go up to a gal and throw her down – you'd be up Shit Creek without a canoe. But if she bumps into *you*, well now, that's different.'

'You shouldn't have done it. Not to her.'

'Christ on a hunchin' crutch, man, you turning into a fag on me? First it's Bennett you're sticking up for, now it's this Beth. You lost your sense of humor?' He shook his head, looking disgusted. 'And here I was, just about to give you my plan that's one-hundred percent guaranteed to get you in the sack with Bennett.'

'I've already heard it: you hold her down, I...' He found himself unable to say, 'fuck her'.

'Fuck her?' Nate said for him. 'Nothing so crude, dingus. That'd be rape. We'd go to *el slammer* for that. No no no. What I've got in mind is seduction.'

Bill grinned as if he thought Nate was crazy. 'A plan guaranteed to work?'

'One hundred percent.'

'I'll believe it when it works,' he said, feeling a tight eagerness inside. Christ, what if he *could* somehow seduce Miss Bennett? 'Let's have it.'

'In the art of seduction, Billy my lad, the trick is to get yourself alone with the seducee and let nature take its course.'

'Sure.'

Nate tilted back his head and shut his eyes. 'Our romance begins with a flat tire. You happen to be nearby and rush to the aid of the stranded motorist.' He opened one eye and looked at Bill. 'Get it?'

'Here comes Doons.'

'Oh shit! See you later.' Nate dashed away.

'Hold it!' Doons yelled.

Bill laughed, earning a fierce glare from the v.p.

'Stop! Get back here, Houlder!'

Nate kept running, and vanished around a corner.

'Prick,' Doons muttered. Then he fixed his eyes on Bill. 'Wipe that grin off your face, Kearny.'

Beth sat in the office, waiting. She breathed deeply, trying to calm herself, but the thought of facing Mr Doons was too terrifying. Her hands felt cold and numb. Goosebumps made the light hair on her arms stand up. Her cheerleading sweater, under her arms, was soaked with perspiration. Droplets even rolled down her sides, wetting her bra.

This was worse than waiting for a doctor's exam, and she'd thought nothing could be that bad.

Finally, the bell rang, ending the lunch period.

Won't be long now.

She pressed her hands between her thighs to warm them.

That creep, Nate. It was all his fault.

She heard voices, laughter, and banging lockers from the hallway.

What would happen if she just got up and walked out? Wouldn't help. Doons'd send a call slip to her next class – or go over, himself, and drag her out.

How? He doesn't know my name, does he?

He could find out, easily enough.

Besides, sooner or later he would see her between classes or something, and grab her. But maybe he'd forget about her, by that time.

Mrs Houston glanced at her. Beth smiled, but her mouth trembled. The woman returned to her typing.

She won't try to stop me...

The door opened and Mr Doons came in. 'Into my office, Elizabeth.'

He *does* know my name!

She got up. On weak legs, she walked ahead of him, past Mrs Houston's desk, and through the open door.

Doons shut the door. He stepped around a big desk and sat on a swivel chair. Leaning forward, he planted his elbows on the green blotter. 'Take a seat,' he said.

She sat on a folding chair across from him. Her chin trembled. She pressed her lips together.

'Now, Elizabeth, tell me what happened.'

'I was just ... I was talking to Aleshia and I backed up and bumped into him.'

'Nate Houlder.'

'Yes.'

'Then what?'

'We fell down.'

'Houlder pushed you down?'

'We ... just fell.'

'And he wouldn't let you up?'

'No. I mean yes. He held me down.'

'Why?'

'I don't know.'

'What did he do, then?'

145

'Nothing.' Her throat felt tight and achy. She tried to swallow, and almost gagged.

'Where were his hands?'

'Just ... just holding me. I wanted to get up, but he wouldn't let me.'

'Where were his hands?'

'Behind me, I guess.'

'You guess?'

She nodded.

Mr Doons's eyes dropped briefly to her breasts, then returned to her face. His thumb and forefinger rubbed the flesh above his lip. 'Did Houlder touch you anyplace intimate?'

She shook her head.

'Your breasts?'

'*No.*'

'Your genital area or buttocks?'

'No,' she said, her voice husky and quiet.

'You don't sound very sure.'

'He *didn't*!' Tears came to her eyes. She wiped them off with her sleeve.

'I don't like liars, Miss Green.'

'He didn't touch me there!'

'I was told by a witness that he put a hand in your panties.'

'That's a lie!'

His face reddened. 'Are you calling me a liar?'

'No,' she sobbed. 'Not you. The witness. Whoever told you that.'

'It came from a reliable source. Why do you feel that you have to protect Houlder?'

'I'm not!'

'Is he your boyfriend?'

'No!'

'Then why did you let him put a hand inside your pants?'

'I didn't. *He* didn't.'

Doons sighed.

'He *didn't*!'

'Perhaps you just didn't notice. All right, Elizabeth. That'll be all. Have Mrs Houston give you a re-admit slip.'

24

After lunch, Sam drove out on Oakhurst Road. He slowed down, passing the Horner house. Only its chimney and half a wall remained standing. The rest of the house had fallen to a charred pile of debris.

Next door, the Sherwood house seemed almost cheerful.

Wouldn't be such a bad place, Sam thought, if somebody'd move in and fix it up.

Driving past the house of Clara Hayes, he saw the morning newspaper on her front lawn. He wondered why she hadn't picked it up yet.

Across the road, he saw a group of brightly-clad golfers on the green of the third hole. One of the men waved at him. Though he only glimpsed the man, he tapped his horn twice in greeting.

Then he tried to remember what he'd been thinking about before the golfer waved.

Something about the Sherwood house?

Wouldn't make a bad fixer-upper.

Maybe Morley could sell it to the Horners, if they ever showed up again. Assuming Hank isn't the one who killed Dexter.

Though Sam knew little about Hank Horner, he saw

no reason to believe the man was involved. The burning house and disappearance of the family were certainly not proof.

Strange, though, that it happened the day after Dex got killed. Maybe a connection, but not the one Berney was hoping for. Maybe both men had the same enemy. Maybe whoever chopped up Dex...

Sam moaned as he again saw himself lift the toilet seat and look down at Dexter's floating head. He took a deep breath.

'Whoever killed Dex killed the Horners,' he said aloud. The sound of his voice drove the memories away. 'Burnt the house to destroy any physical evidence he – she – they left behind. So where are the bodies? If they're not in the house...' He clucked his tongue as he thought. 'If they're not in the house...?' he repeated. 'Buried out back?'

He remembered what was 'out back' of the Horner house.

Oakhurst Cemetery.

Dendron could wait. If he didn't see Thelma this afternoon, he'd find her tonight.

Slowing, he swung the car into a U-turn and sped back toward the cemetery.

The wrought-iron gates of Oakhurst Cemetery stood open. Sam drove through, and followed the narrow road to the parking lot. Except for a black Coup de Ville and a pick-up truck, the lot was deserted. He parked, and climbed out. Walking into the wind, he watched dry leaves tumble and skitter toward him.

The grass on the rolling fields looked bright green in

the sunlight and he thought, with a pang of nostalgia, what a great day this would be for touch football.

A great day, but not a great place.

The door of the cemetery office opened, and a tall gray-haired man stepped out, his suit jacket flapping in the wind. When he saw Sam, his head tipped back and he smiled. He changed course, slightly, and approached.

'Wyatt.'

'Brandner,' Sam said, shaking hands with his old friend.

'What's a nice fellow like you doing in a place like this?'

'I was about to ask you the same thing,' Sam told him.

'Too windy for tennis. Perfect weather for a Bloody Mary, though. How about joining me?'

'Believe me, I'd like to.'

'Busy detecting, I presume.'

'Right.'

The smile left Brandner's lean face. 'Rotten about Dexter. I hear you're the one who found him.'

'Yeah.'

'He was a good man. I guess you'll be here Sunday for the interment.'

'Yeah.'

'Christ, it gets to me when a guy I know ... Well, business is business, I guess. One of these fine days, I'm gonna chuck all this and buy me a bar.'

'Hope you do it soon.'

'How about a partnership?'

'Just tell me when.'

'I guess you must have plenty socked away, from all your graft.'

'A bundle. Right now, though, I've got some snooping to do.'

'Snoop away.'

'I know you wouldn't be caught dead here at night...'

'Touché!'

'But do you know if anything unusual happened here last night?'

Brandner rubbed his chin, and shook his head. 'You don't mean the fire, I take it.'

'The Horners' bodies weren't found.'

'You're thinking they segued into my bone orchard?'

'I'd like to find out. If they were murdered, the killer probably didn't move them far.'

'Why move them at all?'

'Don't ask me. If they weren't in the house, though, where are they?'

'Visiting Aunt Mary?'

'Do you want to come along?' Sam asked.

'Where?'

'I want to check the area in back of their house.'

'I suppose my Bloody Marys can wait.'

They walked, side by side, to the far end of the parking lot, then up a grassy slope, passing between well-tended grave sites.

'To think I used to play here as a wee child,' Brandner said. 'My cousin cured me of that. We were playing tag, one day, blithely scampering among the graves – did I ever tell you this?'

Sam had heard the story a couple of times before, over drinks, but he shook his head.

'She – my cousin – tripped in a gopher hole. She looked down the hole, and kept looking and looking. I

151

said, "Hey, what're you doing?" The little bitch said,
"There's somebody down there winking at me."'

'Did you take a look?'

'Are you kidding? I ran like hell, and wouldn't come
near this place for a year. Christ, I still get the
creeps whenever I see a gopher hole around here. And
there're plenty. I often suspect the little buggers are
carnivorous.'

'You'd better buy that bar soon.'

'Don't I know it. This business is not for the squeam-
ish. Should've sold out when my father died.'

'Why didn't you?'

'A sense of family obligation, I suppose. Obligation
gets to you every time.'

Ahead, through the trees and monuments, Sam saw
the wrought-iron fence of the cemetery boundary. The
dark chimney of the Horner house stood not far beyond
it.

Brandner frowned. 'You think someone chucked their
bodies over my fence?'

'Maybe buried them over here.'

'A logical place, I suppose.'

'Any recent graves over here?'

'Open ones? No. And I think Willie would've noticed if
someone had been digging. He's a sot, but he's not deaf
and blind.'

'It's a big cemetery.'

'He makes regular rounds. He's *supposed* to, anyhow.'

They reached the fence. Sam looked through at the
rubble. The wind carried a pungent odor of burnt wood.

With his back to the fence, he looked down its length.
The gravestones, monuments, and clusters of trees and

bushes offered plenty of places to conceal bodies or crouch, out of sight, to dig a hole.

'I hope you're wrong about this,' Brandner said.

'It's worth a look.'

They began walking alongside the fence, occasionally separating while one inspected the ground behind a tree or gravestone.

'If these Horners *were* murdered,' Brandner said, 'you would have to suspect they were done in by the one who killed Dexter.'

'I've thought of that.'

'Thought you might've. Has it also occurred to you that we're now directly behind the Sherwood house?'

'What about it?'

'Seems a bit funny, to me, that two families, right next door to each other, should get slaughtered.'

'Fifteen years apart.'

'How many mass murders have we had in Ashburg? Two. Fifteen years apart, but side by side. Seems funny to me. I think, if I were looking for the Horners' bodies – which I apparently am, thanks to you – I'd take a look in the Sherwood house.'

'I may do that.'

'Fine. Let's forget all this and ... well well well.'

As Brandner crouched behind a tombstone, Sam rushed to his side. 'There were bodies here, all right,' his friend said.

On the grass by the tombstone lay a collapsed tube of pink latex.

'Live ones,' Sam added.

'In my experience,' said Brandner, 'corpses rarely use rubbers.'

153

25

Glendon Morley got up from his desk as a young couple entered his real estate office. At first, their appearance put him off.

The woman, though somewhat pretty, wore no make-up. Her thick brown hair was drawn back in a pony tail, and she wore a loose, faded dress that looked home-made. She seemed clean, though. Glendon guessed that she wasn't a poverty-stricken gal from the hill country, after all – just an artsy-fart who wanted to look like one.

The man beside her was a giant, well over six feet tall with unruly black hair and eyes so intense that they made Glendon nervous. He wore a tan, corduroy jacket that badly needed to be pressed. Beneath it was a T-shirt decorated by a hideous, troll-like character. Printed below its leering face were the words, 'Trust Me'. He wore blue jeans, and a pair of Adidas running shoes.

'Mr Morley?' the giant asked, offering a hand.

'Yes *sir*,' Glendon said. He shook the man's powerful hand, and smiled at the woman.

'I'm Harold Krug. This is my wife, Seana.'

'Pleased to meet you,' Glendon said. 'House hunting?'

Harold grinned. It was a one-sided, play-evil grin one might use to tease a child. 'I think we found what we want.'

'Excellent. Have a seat, won't you? Could I get you some coffee?'

'Yeah. Black for me.'

'How about you, Seana?'

"I'd prefer tea, if you have some.'

'Sure thing. Tea it is.' Leaving them at his desk, he stepped to the card table in the rear. As he poured the drinks, he tried to size up Harold and Seana. They were from out of town, he was sure of that. They dressed weird – kind of like college kids he'd seen at some of the JC football games. They didn't seem poor or stupid, but Harold obviously didn't earn his keep as a legitimate business man. Teachers? That had to be it.

'Where you from?' he asked, approaching with the tea and two cups of coffee.

'Maine,' Harold said.

'Whew. Long way from the home ground.'

Harold smiled and nodded. He was slouched in the chair beside Glendon's desk, a foot propped over his knee.

'And you're planning to settle down here in Ashburg?'

'For a while.'

Glendon handed the styrene cup of tea to Seana, the coffee to Harold. 'Couldn't pick a nicer little town. I've lived here all my life, myself, and I don't mind telling you wild horses couldn't drag me away from here. What do you do?' he asked Harold.

'I write books.'

'Oh?' He tried to keep his smile as he saw the chances of a sale sink away. 'What sort of books do you write?'

'Occult thrillers.'

'Oh? Like *The Exorcist*?'

'Something like that.'

'My daughter saw that movie.' He chuckled. 'It scared her silly.'

'I'm interested in the Sherwood house.'

'You're interested in buying it?'

Harold nodded, and poked a cigarette into his mouth. 'Okay if I smoke?'

'Sure. No problem. I'm a cigar smoker, myself.' He pushed a spotless, glass ashtray over the desk toward Harold.

'Thanks.'

'So, you plan to do a little first-hand research for one of your books, Harold?'

'Partly that.' The cigarette bounced in his lips. 'We hear it's in bad shape. Is it liveable?'

'Sure. No problem, there.'

'What's the asking price?'

Glendon told him.

Harold scowled through his smoke. 'Sounds reasonable enough. What do you think, Seana?'

She arched an eyebrow, and nodded.

'Most banks will want about fifteen percent down.'

'No problem,' said Harold, grinning.

The man's casual attitude toward the price encouraged Glendon. Maybe this was a writer with money.

'Well,' Glendon said, 'shall we go over and have a look-see?'

'Let's go.'

As they prepared to leave the office, Glendon asked, 'You do know what happened there?'

'Not as much as I'd like to.'

'How did you hear about it?'

'I've been corresponding with a fellow from your high school. The librarian there. Name of Nick Carlson.'

'Oh?'

'He says it's been deserted since the murders.'

'That's right.' Glendon turned off the lights, and held the door open. Harold and Seana stepped out. He locked the door. 'My car's just over there.'

They headed for the brown Fleetwood.

'Nobody in this town's too interested in living there, after what happened.'

'Sherwood was the high school principal?'

'Vice principal, I think. I tell you, this town was mighty shook up by the killings. Never did find out who did them, so I think about half the folks were just holding their breath, waiting for the killer to strike again. He never did, though. Whoever he was, he must've moved on.'

Glendon unlocked the passenger door, and opened it. 'Plenty of room in the front,' he said. They climbed in, and Glendon went around to the driver's door. 'Are you planning to write about the house, Harold?'

'I'm more interested in the atmosphere, just now.' He made that play-evil grin again. 'I write better when I'm frightened. I like to scare myself.'

'Well, this place should certainly fill the bill.' Glendon started the car, and pulled away from the curb. 'Do you write too, Seana?'

'Not I. One neurotic in the family is enough.'

'Will this be your first house?'

'We have one near Portland,' she said.

'Has it sold yet?'

'Oh, we're keeping it.'

'That's our home base,' Harold explained.

'So you're not planning to make Ashburg your home?'

'For a year or two.'

'Well, this'll make a dandy fixer-upper. Do a few improvements, you should be able to sell it at a nice profit. Your living in it should take the curse off, and folks won't be afraid to buy.'

'If we don't get butchered,' Harold added, eyes twinkling.

Glendon laughed loudly. 'Oh, I doubt you have to worry on that score.'

He swung his Fleetwood onto the driveway. Weeds had pushed through the loose gravel, and the yard was overgrown. He'd been careless, lately, about keeping the place up. Wouldn't have to give it any more thought, though, if these folks took it off his hands.

He would be proved right about his investment, too. Everyone had said he was crazy when he bought the Sherwood house at public auction – for next to nothing. He'd finally almost decided they were right. But if these Krugs bought the place, he'd be doing very well indeed. Nobody laughs at a 500 percent profit.

'Lawn needs some work,' he admitted, shutting off the engine.

'Needs a tractor,' Harold said.

Glendon laughed. 'At least you won't be bothered by noisy neighbors. You've got your graveyard out back, and the golf course in front. Mrs Hayes, over there, is an elderly lady who keeps to herself. And I'm sure nobody'll be building on the Horner lot for some time.'

They climbed out of the car. 'Electricity's not on,' Glendon said, and raised the lid of his trunk. He took out a powerful, battery-operated lantern. Then he led the way through the weeds. Smiling back, he noticed how the wind pushed Seana's dress against her body, molding it to her breasts and slim legs as if the fabric were wet. Not a bad looking woman, he thought, if only she'd fix herself up a bit.

He paused at the foot of the veranda. The banister's white paint was curling and flaking like the dead skin of a sunburn. 'She could probably stand a coat of paint,' he said.

Harold grinned. 'Looks just great to me.'

They climbed the steps. 'I guess,' Glendon said, 'if the place was all kept up neat and pretty, it wouldn't have that atmosphere you're talking about.'

'Very true, Mr Morley.'

'Call me Glendon, Harold.'

Harold nodded.

Glendon pushed a key into the padlock. 'We had to put some extra security on the place,' he said. 'Otherwise, there's no telling what might go on in here. Kids, you know. A few got in, a couple years back. Didn't do much harm, though. Painted up the walls a bit, is all.' He removed the padlock, and fit a key into the door's lockface. 'If you take the place, I'll send a man out and have the boards taken off the windows. Windows are all intact, by the way.'

He opened the door. Light from outside spilled into

the foyer, and lit the foot of the stairway. 'We can leave the door open. Give us a little extra light.'

He frowned, stepping inside. The stale air smelled of paint. Had someone broken in again?

'Is it supposed to be haunted?' Harold asked.

'Everybody says so.' Glendon hadn't heard anything to that effect, but he knew the man wanted atmosphere so he elaborated. 'They say the ghosts of the Sherwoods walk the rooms at midnight.'

'Hope so,' said Harold.

Glendon turned on his lantern. 'The living room's over here.' He led the way. The smell of paint grew stronger. In the entry, he shined his wide beam into the room. He gasped, took a quick step backward, and bumped into Harold.

'*Bars* on the windows?' Harold asked.

'Something's wrong here.'

The front door banged shut.

Whirling around, he glimpsed a pale figure at the door. He shined his light on the motionless shape of a man. A policeman? The uniform was dark with stains like dry blood. The face under the brim of the cowboy hat looked vaguely familiar. Old, wrinkled, womanly, sagging like a poorly fitted mask.

'Who are you?' Glendon muttered.

'Harry?' Seana gasped.

Harold grabbed her shoulder, and pulled her close to him. 'Is there a back way out of here?' he asked.

'Locked,' Glendon said. 'On the outside.'

One of the arms moved away from the silent man's side. The hand gripped a hatchet.

Seana groaned.

'No way out?' Harold asked.

'He's standing in front of it.'

'Give me that.' He yanked the lantern from Glendon's hand, and threw it toward the door.

'What're you...?' Glendon stopped his voice as the light crashed and went out. For a few moments, his eyes retained the beam's after-image. Then all he saw was blackness.

'Blind man's bluff,' whispered Harold. His voice wasn't close.

'Don't leave me!' Glendon cried.

Light blasted his eyes as the front door flew open. In the glare from outside, he glimpsed Harold and Seana on the stairway, heading up, *leaving* him!

'*Wait!*'

But then he saw his chance. The awful figure with the hatchet was gone. Had he run out?

Glendon sprang for the door.

It crashed shut in front of him.

He threw himself against it, clawing the knob, sobs shaking him as he realized that the man hadn't run out the door, at all, but only hid behind it and now was coming at him in the darkness.

'No please,' he cried. 'Don't. Please!'

Something brushed against his hair. He jumped, bashing his forehead against the door.

'Please,' he sobbed. 'Don't...'

Something smacked his back, just below the shoulder blade. It split him, burning. The *hatchet*! It pulled out. It went away.

'*No!*' he shrieked.

He tugged the door, but it wouldn't open. He felt a

sharp jolt, heard a *thunk*. Pain ripped across his back. He could feel it, actually feel the hatchet head inside his back, wedged between his ribs, feel it rock as the man tried to pull it out.

His legs went numb.

He fell facedown.

The hatchet went away.

Again, it chopped into his back. And again. Though the pain was a steady roar in his head, part of his mind seemed calm, almost rational. This must be Jim Sherwood, it told him. Jim's ghost? He thinks I'm a trespasser. If I can just explain I'm his old friend Glen . . .

Another burst of pain shook him.

The hatchet chopped and chopped in the blackness. It struck his back, his shoulders, his buttocks. Glendon wanted to shout for the man to stop.

His voice wouldn't work.

Who does he think I *am*?

A singsong voice from his childhood came back.

I'm nobody, who are you?

Harold pulled his wife by the hand through the blackness.

'What'll we do?' she whispered.

'Shhhh.'

He walked slowly, feeling the wall.

So hard to believe this was happening to them. Trapped in a deserted house by an ax-wielding maniac. He'd seen such situations countless times in the movies, read about them in so many books, written them himself more than once.

Incidental characters, in this circumstance, never

survived. The main character, though, usually found a way to triumph. Didn't seem completely fair.

In his next book, he ought to handle it differently. Hell, though, *somebody* has to bite the dust.

Not us!

He found an open door, pulled Seana inside, and shut it. He felt the knob. Found a lock button, pushed it. The lock made a feeble click.

'That won't ... He's got a hatchet.'

'I know.' Harold found the light switch, and flicked it. Nothing happened. He took a matchbook from a pocket of his corduroy jacket, flipped open its cover, and peeled out a cardboard match. He struck it.

In the shimmering light, he saw that they'd taken refuge in a bathroom.

Seana sat down on the toilet seat, and rubbed her face.

Harold stepped to the sink. He smiled nervously at himself in the medicine cabinet mirror. The reflection of his face, quivering with deep shadows, looked demonic. He quickly lowered his eyes to the sink. He turned a faucet handle. It squawked, but no water came.

'Can't flood him out,' he whispered, grinning.

He pulled open the medicine cabinet. Its shelves were bare. The flame singed his fingers. He dropped the match into the sink, and lit another.

A large tub. A shower curtain rod with metal rings but no curtain.

At the far end of the tub was the bathroom's only window. No light came through. A wrought-iron grate covered it on the inside. 'What are the *bars* for?' he muttered.

'To keep us in,' said Seana.

'This guy does plan ahead.'

'I'm glad you haven't lost your sense of humor.'

'It's always the last to go.'

'What'll we do?'

He shook out his match. Whispering in the darkness, he said, 'Did you bring your gun?'

'Oh Harold.'

'No, I didn't think...' He jumped as something crashed against the door. '*Jeezus!*' Rushing through the darkness, he bumped into Seana. They both fell. 'Here. *Here.*' He pushed the matchbook into her hand. 'Light 'em for me.'

'What're you...'

Another blow shocked the door.

Harold scurried off Seana. Standing, be jerked open his belt. He tugged it off.

'Light.'

Seana struck a match. In its wavering glow, he saw a splintered gash in the door panel. He stepped to the side. The hatchet struck again, shaking the door. A corner of its head appeared. It hit again, spraying splinters, the hatchet head breaking through the door. Harold hooked his belt under it, looped over its top, and yanked. The hatchet sprang loose. He pulled it in.

'You got it!' Seana cried.

'Into the tub, quick!'

Grabbing the weapon, he rushed to Seana. He clutched her arm. The match went out. He pulled her toward the tub. They crawled over its side.

'Lie down,' he whispered.

'But...'

'He's got a gun.'

'You sure?'

'*Yes.*'

He pressed her to the bottom of the tub, and crouched at her head, hatchet ready. His heart thudded so hard he thought he might vomit. He took deep breaths.

They waited.

'Maybe he doesn't have bullets,' Seana whispered.

'I'm not going out there to find out.'

'What'll we do?'

'Wait.'

26

Driving away from the Oakhurst Cemetery, Sam recalled Brandner's suggestion: 'If I were looking for the Horners' bodies ... I'd take a look in the Sherwood house.'

It seemed like a good idea.

He might, at least, make a quick tour of its outside – check the doors, see if anything seemed out of place. But as he approached the house, he saw the Morley Realty car parked in front. Not much point looking around, he decided, if Glendon's in the house. The real estate man would be certain to report anything he found amiss.

So Sam didn't stop.

Nor did he stop when he noticed, again, that Clara's newspaper still remained on her lawn.

He'd spent a long time at the cemetery. After a thorough search of the area near the north fence, he and Brandner made a quick inspection of the rest of the grounds. Along the way, he questioned Benny, the grounds keeper, and learned nothing of importance. The entire procedure had taken nearly two hours; if he met another delay, he might as well forget about Dendron and simply wait for Thelma to return.

He didn't want to wait.

He wanted to make the trip on the chance of catching Thelma at her mother's house. He wanted to make it, even if he failed to meet her.

He was very nervous.

I'm not going to stop, he thought. No reason to be nervous, because I'm not going to stop. When I get to the Sleepy Hollow Inn, I'll just keep driving. I've got a job to do.

What about afterwards?

No!

Wouldn't hurt to stop and thank Melodie for the help. If it weren't for her call, you wouldn't have the first idea where to find Thelma.

I'll thank her by phone.

I can't see her again. Can't.

As the motel came into view, Sam's heart hammered so hard and fast he felt dizzy. He scanned the area, but didn't see her. He stared at the office windows. He turned his head, looking for as long as possible before he left the motel behind.

He hadn't so much as glimpsed her. The loss made him ache inside, like a child whose birthday was forgotten.

I can always stop on the way back, he told himself.

But I won't.

I'd better not.

Couldn't hurt to thank her, though.

Yes it could. It could hurt a lot.

The house at 354 Tenth Street in Dendron looked small and well-kept. A picket fence enclosed its neatly trimmed lawn. A Honda Civic was parked in its driveway.

Sam stopped at the curb and climbed out. He hurried toward the front door, eager to conclude the hunt that had occupied so much of his time for the past two days. He didn't expect resistance. He expected her to play it cool, even if she were responsible for Dexter's murder. As he reached the door, however, doubts crept in. Should he notify the local police? He'd have to phone them, anyway, if it came down to an arrest.

That could wait.

For all he knew, Thelma had already returned to Ashburg.

He stood off to the side, as a precaution, and pressed the doorbell. He heard it ring. His hand lowered to his revolver.

The door opened and a petite, white-haired woman looked out at him. 'Yes?' she asked.

'Is Thelma here?'

'Why, yes she is. You must be Mr Wyatt.'

He nodded.

'Marjorie called. She told us to expect you, but we thought you'd be here ages ago.'

'I had some other business,' he said, wishing now that he hadn't delayed so long.

'Won't you come in?'

He followed her into the living room. Thelma, sitting in a rocker, watched him over the rim of a cocktail glass. Her half-shut eyes had the same lazy insolence Sam knew from her photo. She looked much older, though: thin, with a sallow complexion and harsh lines.

'I wasn't so hard to find, was I?' She smirked and took a drink. 'Mother, how about disappearing for a bit?'

'Would Mr Wyatt care for a drink?' asked the older woman.

'No he wouldn't,' Thelma answered.

'There's no call to be rude, darling.'

'No call to be polite. This man wants to bust me for killing Dexter.'

'I'm not here to bust you,' Sam said.

'I'll believe that when I see it.'

'I just want to...'

'I know, ask a few questions. Good-*bye* Mother.'

Looking peeved, the old woman scurried from the room.

'Okay,' said Thelma, 'what do you want to know?'

'Let's start at the beginning.'

'How about getting it over with? You've already got my story from Elmer and Marjorie and Ticia and God-only-knows who else.'

'I'd like to hear it from you.'

She sighed. 'Elmer's right about you. Okay. I get into town Tuesday afternoon, check in at my sister's house. Have supper with them, then make my merry way to the Sunset Lounge where I meet my old friend Elmer. We hoist a few, then take off in his Volvo, spread his blanket on the eighth hole of the golf course and go humpy-humpy. Okay? The automatic sprinklers go on, and we get drenched. Never fuck on a golf course.

'Elmer takes me back to Marjorie's, and I hit the sack. Wednesday, I meet Elmer for lunch. He takes me shopping, so I can pick up a few items for Marjorie. I eat supper with the family, then take off with Ticia for the Sunset. We meet Elmer there, and I meet Joe.'

'Joe who?'

'Joe Schmow, who the hell knows? So me and Joe go off together for a merry time.'

'When?'

She smirked. 'Eleven or twelve. I didn't clock out. Who knows?'

'Do you know where you went?'

'Not to the golf course, you can bet.'

'Where?'

'Here's the good part, the part you've been waiting for. You figure I went over to Dexter's place and chopped him up, right?'

'Did you?'

'Hate to disappoint you.'

'Where did you go?'

'Stiff City. Oakhurst Cemetery.' She swirled her ice cubes, and took a drink. 'You haven't lived till you've gone humpy-humpy in the graves. It adds a certain thrill. Makes it terribly exciting, like screwing in public without the scandal.'

'How long were you there?' Sam asked.

'Oh, an hour.'

'Nobody can prove you were there.'

'Only Joe. I'm sure, if it's necessary, we can dig him up.'

'You'd better hope so.'

She shook her head, smiling with one side of her face. 'I don't imagine it'll be necessary.'

'Why not?'

'Oh, I saw something that will interest you.' She took another drink. 'Guess what I saw.'

'Why don't you just tell me?'

'I'd have told you, long ago, if you hadn't insisted on my repeating all that useless trivia.'

'What did you see at the cemetery?'

'Not a what, but a who.'

'Okay.'

'I saw Dexter.' She licked her lips and took another drink. 'It was only by the purest luck that I happened to see him. If I'd been under Joe, at the time ... Most men prefer it that way, do you?'

Sam didn't answer.

Thelma chuckled. 'They like to feel they're controlling the action, get insecure if the gal's on top. At any rate, Joe isn't that way. So I was merrily riding him along, and I happened to be facing that creepy old house where all those people got murdered – the Sherman house?'

'Sherwood.'

'At any rate, I happened to be looking that way and saw Dexter go in the back door.'

'He *entered* the Sherwood house?'

'That's what I said. He went in, and I didn't see him come out.'

'Are you sure it was Dex?'

'I couldn't see his face, obviously. But he was Dexter's size, and wearing a police uniform and Stetson just like Dexter's. Oh, it was him all right.'

'Why didn't you notify someone?'

'Why should I? His business is no business of mine.

Especially now.' She sucked an ice cube into her mouth. It muffled her voice as she said, 'God rest his soul.'

27

'Hey jack-off!'

Bill ignored Nate's voice, and finished stuffing his books into his overflowing locker. He let go. As the books started to avalanche, he slammed the metal door. He turned to his friend. 'Doons catch you yet?'

'Doons couldn't catch shit if he tripped over it.'

'Where'd you hide?'

'The girls' locker room.'

'Sure.'

'I tell you, my dick's been hard so long I'm starting to take it for granite.'

Bill shook his head. 'You must've spent all afternoon thinking up that one.'

'Nah. I'm a natural wit.'

They walked up the crowded hallway, Bill watching as Nate collided with students in his way. Girls and smaller boys only. When boys larger than Nate drew near, he sidestepped out of range.

Bill followed him across the hall, curious until he saw a large-bosomed blonde ahead. Nate altered course and walked into her.

'Watch it,' she snapped.

'I think you busted my arm!'

173

'Bull-twinkie,' she said.

Nate turned to Bill. 'Busted my arm. Get it? Busted?'

'Very funny.'

'What're you, still pissed off about your sweetie Beth? Or is it Miss Bennett? Look, it's time we get on the ball with Bennett, you know what I mean? It's now or never, do or die, shit or get off the commode. Hey hey, look who's here.'

Bill saw Eric Prince walking up the hall.

'Hey dork-face,' Nate called.

Eric saw him, and stopped.

'Hey dingle-berry, come here.'

Eric took a single step forward. Several students pushed past him.

Nate stopped in front of him. 'Trick or treat,' he said.

'I haven't got...'

'How much *have* you got?'

Eric shrugged.

'Well check, turd-head.'

He pushed a bandaged hand into a front pocket of his trousers, and brought out a comb and handkerchief.

'Try the other pocket.'

Wincing, he shifted a load of books to his left hand.

'What's the matter with your hand?' Nate asked.

'I cut it,' Eric said, reaching into a pocket.

'Sure. I bet you wore a hole in it jacking off.'

Eric's right hand appeared. He held it out to Nate, and opened it. 'This is all I've got,' he said.

Bill glanced at the nickels and pennies.

'That's all?' Nate asked.

'Yeah.'

'How'm I supposed to exist on such a pittance? Answer me that.'

'I don't know.'

'Keep it,' Nate said, and slapped his hand up. The change flew, several coins striking a nearby girl in the face.

'Come on, Bill.'

As they walked away, Bill looked back. Eric was still standing where they'd left him, surrounded by talking, shoving, laughing students who passed him like a stream swirling around a rock. For a moment, Bill felt a little sorry for the kid. Then he saw a corner of Eric's mouth twist into a sneer. A chill prickled the back of his neck, and he turned away.

'Okay, so here's my plan for Bennett.'

'I won't let you flatten her tires,' Bill said. They went outside, and down the concrete stairs. 'Why don't we just forget about her?'

'Hey, you haven't heard my new plan, yet. What we do, we get in my car and wait by the faculty parking lot. When she comes out, we follow her home. How's that sound?'

'I don't know,' Bill said.

'We'll hang back – she'll never be the wiser.'

'What'll we do when we get there?'

'What do you want to do?'

'Nothing.'

'Then that's what we'll do.'

'Then why go at all?'

'So we'll know where she lives, dildo.'

28

From a distance, Eric watched the cheerleaders practice. He was still shaken up by his encounter with Nate,
but he soon forgot about it as the girls leaped and
twirled, and kicked their bare legs.

They all looked so beautiful.

Especially Aleshia. Her slim legs were golden in the
afternoon sunlight. When she whirled around, her
pleated skirt flew high, giving Eric glimpses of her
thighs and green underpants. When she jumped, plunging her arms at the sky, her sweater slid up and
uncovered her belly for an instant.

He knew she didn't wear bras to school.

If only she would jump higher...

Once, she did a cartwheel and the sweater dropped
nearly to her ribs before she whipped to her feet and it
fell again into place. He imagined her doing another
cartwheel, this time her sweater sliding down all the
way and uncovering her small, pale breasts.

He realized he had an erection. Glancing down, he
saw it pushing out his corduroys. He folded his hands in
front of the bulge, and turned his eyes toward Beth.

Though nowhere as pretty as Aleshia, Beth was fairly
cute. Doing the cheers, she seemed more enthusiastic

than the others. Compared to her, the rest of the girls looked lazy, almost bored.

Her arms snapped forward as the voices chanted, 'Push 'em back, push 'em back, waaaay back.' At the cheer's end, she bounded from the ground, arching her back, waving her arms, kicking her feet up high behind her. Eric looked quickly at Aleshia and found her in mid-air, her sweater up, her belly showing pale and smooth.

He imagined sliding his hands up her belly, up under the sweater where it was warm and dark, and taking her breasts in his hands, holding them gently, his palms barely touching the velvet skin.

'Hi Eric!' Beth called, waving at him. 'We're almost done.'

He nodded and yelled, 'Okay.'

A few of the girls huddled around Beth. Eric guessed they were talking about him. He wished he could hear them, but they spoke quietly and the distance was great.

What if they'd seen his bulge?

How could he face Beth, after that?

The girls weren't giggling, though. Soon, they stopped talking and resumed practice.

Eric turned away. He walked along the side of the field, his back to the cheerleaders. Though he wished he could watch them, he didn't want to embarrass himself by getting another erection. So he walked along, listening.

'We are the Spartans, the mighty-mighty Spartans! Everywhere we go-o, people oughtta kno-ow, who we are *so* we tell 'em. We are the Spartans...'

He saw the football team ahead, running a scrimmage. The coach was there, so none of the jerks were likely to try anything with Eric. Just to be safe, though, he turned away and walked toward the school.

He glanced back at the cheerleaders and saw them in a line, kicking their legs high.

Finally, he reached the main building. He sat on the steps to wait for Beth. From there, he could barely hear the chants of the cheerleaders. He watched the girls dance and leap, but they were tiny now, their features less distinct. He found it difficult to tell one from another. Beth, the only stocky girl of the five, was easy to spot, but he couldn't make up his mind which of the others was Aleshia.

As he waited, the coldness of the concrete seeped through his pants. He began to feel as if he were sitting on a slab of ice. Raising himself off the step, he slid his grammar book beneath him. He sat on it. The book felt warm under his buttocks.

Opening his three-ring binder to a blank page, he began to doodle. He drew a revolver, but it turned out crooked, the barrel curving upward as if bent by Superman. His Bowie knife came out well. He inked in drops of blood falling from its blade. Encouraged by his success with the knife, he tried to draw a P-40 Kittyhawk. The fuselage looked good, but he had trouble with the wings and tail. He went ahead, regardless, and drew the shark's mouth on the engine cowling. When he was done, the combat plane looked lopsided but vicious.

On the back of the page, he drew an oblong and imagined it was a girl's torso. Aleshia's torso. He sketched breasts onto it. They were merely two circles with dots in the middle, but as his pen stroked the paper he could almost feel their smooth flesh.

Then he heard voices nearby.

The cheerleaders, done with practice, were wandering in his direction.

With a few swift strokes, he drew a nose between the breasts, a grinning mouth below them. He put ears on the torso, and a patch of scraggly hair on top.

'Okay, see you tonight,' Beth said, breaking away from the group. She headed for Eric, while the other girls continued around the side of the school.

Eric stood up.

'I hope you didn't mind waiting,' Beth said.

'No, it was fun.' He picked up his books, and saw that she had none. 'Do you need anything inside?'

She shook her head, smiling. 'I finished all my homework in study hall.'

'Wish I had.'

They started to walk.

'What've you got?' Beth asked.

'Homework? About six chapters of *Huckleberry Finn*. I fell behind this week.'

'You have Miss Bennett, don't you?'

'Yeah. Fourth period.'

'I've got her first. She'll be at the party, you know.'

'Aleshia's?'

'Yeah. She's the only teacher Aleshia invited. So, what do you think we should wear?'

'I don't know. What do you think?'

'It'd be neat if we could go as a pair. You know, like Laurel and Hardy or the Blues Brothers.'

'How about Tarzan and Jane?'

Laughing, she bumped him with her shoulder. 'That's awful. Besides, we'd freeze.'

'We'll be inside.'

'You go as Tarzan, if you want. I'll wear clothes.'

Eric frowned. 'Actually, I think we should go as something spooky. I mean, it's Halloween. We oughtta dress up as ghosts or vampires or something.'

'You're right,' Beth said. 'Any ideas?'

'I'd like to be something *real* spooky.'

'Like what?'

Eric shrugged.

'It'll have to be something simple,' Beth said as they crossed the deserted faculty parking lot. 'We haven't got much time.'

'Do you have some old, ragged clothes? An old dress or something you can wreck up?'

'I guess so.'

'Great.'

'What's great?'

'What's the scariest thing you can think of?'

She shrugged. 'I don't know. I haven't thought about it. A psycho, I guess. You know, like those guys that rape girls and torture them to death.' She wrinkled her nose at the thought. 'Wouldn't be much fun to dress like that.'

'What about the living dead?'

'Like *Walkers*?'

'I was thinking *Night of the Living Dead*.'

'I never saw that. I heard it's yucky.'

'It's great. Anyway, we can dress up like one of those – if you don't mind looking sloppy.'

'No, that's fine.'

'You want to?'

'Sure. I guess.'

'Okay. So wear a dress you don't need anymore.'

'Is that it?'

'I'll bring along some stuff.' He grinned. 'This'll be great.'

29

Sam turned on his headlights as darkness lowered over the road to Ashburg. He was alone in the patrol car.

No need to bring Thelma back.

He believed her story.

She hadn't killed Dexter. She'd been in the graveyard with Joe, just as she claimed. In Sam's mind, the condom confirmed that. It might've belonged to anyone, of course, but its location fit her story. From the place where they found it, she would've had a clear view of the Sherwood house.

As he sped over the dark road, Sam recalled that Ruthie had seen Dexter drive away from home that night. Around ten-fifteen or ten-thirty, when she went out to her car for cigarettes. Dex might've been on his way to the Sherwood house.

Thelma had seen him there after midnight – seen him go in, and not come out.

What the hell was he doing there?

Off duty, but in uniform.

The bright neon sign of the Sleepy Hollow Inn pulled Sam's thoughts away from the case. He stared at the lighted windows of the office. The curtains were open. He glimpsed movement inside, but couldn't recognize

Melodie. His foot left the gas pedal. It brushed against the brake and started to descend. As he approached the motel driveway, he slammed his palm on the steering wheel, sending a shot of pain up his arm. He forced his foot back to the gas pedal.

For a few moments, he watched the motel in his side mirror. Then he took a curve, and darkness replaced its bright lights.

He imagined Melodie at a lighted window, peering out and seeing his car pass by. Would she feel the same disappointment Sam felt now – the same hungry ache and longing?

Sam shook his head.

Forget Melodie.

Melodie ... *a melodie that's sweetly played in tune*. What the hell is that, a poem?

'That's sweetly played in tune,' he repeated. 'As fair art thou, my bonnie lass, so deep in love am I, and I will love thee still, my dear, till a' the seas gang dry. Sure. Burns. Rabbie Burns. Till a' the seas gang dry.'

He hadn't thought of that poem in ten years. He'd memorized it in college – his junior year – for Donna. God, he'd been crazy about Donna. He'd recited the poem to her, one night by the river, and afterwards they made love together for the first time.

Good old Rabbie Burns.

The memory soured as he remembered Donna dumping him for that jerk, Roy. He'd warned her that Roy was a sadistic sicko, but she'd laughed it off. Claimed it was sour grapes.

Well, he hoped Donna never had to find out the hard way.

Funny he should think of Donna, after all this time. It was the poem – *a melodie that's sweetly played in tune*.

Melodie again.

I hardly know her, he told himself. Why can't I just forget about her?

Think about the case. Dexter. The Sherwood house. Why had Dex gone over there late at night? To meet someone? Then why in uniform? Must've gone on police business, or he would've worn civvies. There'd been no calls to the station that might've taken him there. Maybe someone called him at home.

Clara Hayes? She's next door to the Sherwood house. She and Dexter were old friends. Maybe she saw a prowler, something like that, and asked him to come over.

Sam remembered the newspaper – still on Clara's lawn at mid-afternoon today.

He hadn't seen her at the fire last night.

His foot eased the gas pedal down. Speeding around a curve, he saw a car ahead. As he gained on it, he switched on his flasher. The car pulled aside, and he shot past it.

He drove as fast as he dared, slowing at curves, picking up speed on the straight-aways. Finally, Clara's house came into view. Her porch light was on, and pale light showed through the curtains of her picture window.

Morley's car, he saw, was still parked in the driveway of the Sherwood house.

Pulling onto the road's shoulder, he stopped in front of Clara's place. He switched off his lights, killed his motor, and climbed out. A chilly wind blew against him as he hurried across her lawn. He picked up the *Clarion*. Walking toward her door, he slipped off its rubber band and glanced at the headline: CHIEF BOYANSKI SLAIN.

On the front stoop, hidden behind a shrub, was another newspaper. Sam picked it up and opened it. The Thursday morning *Clarion*.

He pushed the doorbell.

As it rang, he heard an engine start. The car in the Sherwood driveway backed up. It swung onto the road, still in reverse, and sped backwards.

'Hey!' Sam yelled.

With a crunch of metal and glass it slammed into the front of Sam's patrol car.

'Damn it, Morley!'

He leaped from the stoop and raced across the lawn.

Morley's car didn't move.

As he ran toward it, the passenger window rolled down.

'Morley, what the hell are...?'

Two quick gunshots crashed through his words. He dived for the ground. As he hit, Morley's car took off. He drew his revolver and snapped off four shots. Through the roar of his gunfire, he heard three slugs thunk into the car. The last missed. He took careful aim at the distant target, but decided not to shoot again. Too chancy.

Scrambling to his feet, he ran the final yards to his patrol car.

Though the front was smashed in, the engine turned over. He swung onto the road. Far ahead, Morley's car turned right. Sam floored the accelerator.

He tried the headlights. Dead. But the flasher and siren still worked.

As he raced up the road, he grabbed his radio mike. 'Car Five to headquarters.'

'Go ahead Car Five.'

'I'm in pursuit of a brown Fleetwood, just turned right on Maple at Oakhurst. Suspect armed. Shots fired. Any units in the area? Over.'

Easing off the gas, he skidded around the corner onto Maple and spotted the car a block ahead. This was a residential street, cars parked along both curbs, the streetlamps widely spaced leaving deep swaths of darkness in the middle where the spinning red of his flasher made his only light.

His radio crackled. 'Car Three is responding. What's your ten-twenty?'

'Heading west on Maple, approaching Tenth.'

Yards ahead, a tiny white-sheeted figure stepped out from behind a parked car. Sam hit the brakes. He saw the ghost turn toward him and drop its grocery bag. A little witch grabbed the ghost's sheet and pulled.

Sam wrenched his steering wheel to the left.

The parked station wagon looked bloody in his flasher.

He flung up his arms.

Pain blasted through him, but only for an instant.

Chet Goodman, in Car Three, sped up Maple from the east until he spotted a car in the middle of the road. At first, he thought it was coming his way. Then he realized it wasn't moving at all.

Several yards in front of it, he stopped.

The car was nearly invisible beyond the glare of its headlights. He trained his spotlight on it. A brown Fleetwood.

He picked up his mike. 'Car Three to headquarters.'

'Go ahead Car Three.'

'The suspect vehicle is stopped on Maple between Eleventh and Twelfth Streets. No sign of Car Five. I'll give him a minute to catch up.'

He aimed the spotlight at the windshield, and saw no one.

Removing his Browning from its clamp, he climbed from the car and crouched behind its open door. He pumped a cartridge into the chamber and aimed his shotgun at the Fleetwood's windshield.

'Trouble, officer?' asked a voice behind him.

He looked over his shoulder and a tall, smiling man shot him in the face.

30

'Yee gad!' cried the woman in the doorway.

Eric moaned at her. She shook her head, chuckling, and held out a tray of candy bars.

'I'm not a trick-or-treater,' he told her.

'You always dress this way?'

'I'm here for Beth.'

'Oh! You must be Eric. Please come in. Beth'll be ready in a minute.'

Eric entered the house.

'Martin!' the woman called.

A man with a dish towel came out of the kitchen. When he saw Eric, he made a face and said, 'Yuck.'

'This is Eric Prince, Beth's date for the party.'

'Hi Eric.' Martin stepped toward him frowning with concern. 'You feeling okay?' he asked, shaking hands. 'You look like death warmed over.'

'It's just burnt cork,' Eric explained. 'And some Vampire Blood.'

'They're supposed to be corpses,' the woman said.

'The living dead.'

Martin nodded, pursing his lips as he studied the costume. Eric looked down at himself. The front of his dirty, torn shirt was untucked. His knee showed through a split in his slacks. Through a rent in the other leg, his thigh was visible. Maybe he'd ripped his clothes too much: he didn't want Beth's parents to think him indecent. He wished he hadn't torn the shirt away from his left nipple. The old sports jacket he'd bought at the thrift shop nearly covered it, though.

'I'd say you look very corpse-like,' Martin finally said.

'Thank you.'

At that moment, Beth came into the room. 'Oh wow,' she said. 'You look fantastic!'

'You, too.'

She shrugged. 'It's the best I could do. Did you bring something for my face?'

Eric took a burnt cork and tube of Vampire Blood from his pocket.

'We'd better get back to the dishes,' said her mother. 'You two have a good time.' To Beth, she said, 'Twelve o'clock.'

'Okay.'

'Have fun,' her father said. 'Nice to meet you, Eric.'

'Nice to meet you,' Eric muttered.

He watched them leave. Then he turned to Beth and smiled.

'You'd better fix me up,' she said.

'Now?'

'Might as well. Are my clothes all right?'

'Fine,' he said. Her white blouse was stretched tightly across her full breasts. Its sleeves left her wrists bare. Her green, pleated skirt hung below her knees. She wore old, scuffed loafers. 'It won't hurt to get 'em dirty?' Eric asked.

'We were just gonna give them to Goodwill. They're crummy old things.' She scanned Eric's outfit, grinning. 'Not as crummy as yours, but we can fix that.'

'Yeah,' he said, and blushed.

'Okay, how about doing my face?'

'Well,' he said, offering her the cork. 'You can use this to mess yourself up.'

'You do it.'

She stepped close to him. He smelled a mild, sweet perfume that made his mouth go dry.

'If you want,' he mumbled.

'I want.'

He brushed the charred cork lightly under her eye, but little came off. 'I need to burn it.' He lit a match, and held it to the cork. The charred stub caught fire. He puffed it out, and waited for it to cool.

Beth watched his eyes as he blackened her pale skin. He rubbed smudges under her eyes, heavy lines running down from the sides of her nose to the corners of her mouth. Her constant gaze made him nervous, at first, but soon he began to like it. He shaded her cheeks and chin. 'There.'

'Now the blood.'

Squeezing the plastic tube, he dribbled the syrupy red fluid onto the corners of her mouth. It trickled down her chin. Before a drop could fall to the floor, he smeared it with his fingers.

'More,' she said.

He squirted the blood onto his fingertips, and spread it over her mouth and cheeks and chin. Her skin felt slippery and smooth.

'There,' he said.

Beth took his hand, and wiped it on the belly of her blouse. 'Let's have a look.'

They went to a mirror over the fireplace.

'Fantastic!' she said. 'Boy, aren't we a pair?'

'Yeah. *You* look worse than *me*.'

Still gazing at the mirror, she messed up her hair until it stuck out in wild disarray and strands hung over her face. Then she did the same for Eric.

'That's better, huh?' she asked.

'Great.'

'Let's go.'

They went outside, and cut across Beth's yard to the sidewalk.

'Burrrr,' Beth said.

'Want my jacket?'

'No. Thanks, though. I've got work to do.'

'Hmmm?'

As they walked along, she tugged the front of her blouse out of her skirt. She studied the effect, then tucked one side back in. Picking up her skirt, she yanked the hem. It didn't give.

'Do you have a knife or something?' she asked.

'I have the one I used.' He took out a small pocket knife, opened a blade, and handed it to her.

'Oh, this is good.' She cut through the hem. Clamping the knife between her teeth, she tore a long rip up the front of her skirt.

'Just a minute,' she said. They stopped under a street light. Beth pinched the shoulder of her blouse, pushed the knife into the fabric to start a tear, then hooked her fingers into the hole and jerked. The cloth split. When she finished, her left sleeve hung off her shoulder, still attached to the blouse only at her armpit. 'How's that?'

Her shoulder looked round and glossy in the street light. 'Great,' Eric said.

'One more rip, I think.' She lowered her head, turning it as she studied her front. 'The question is, where?'

'Anywhere.'

'I don't want my bra to show. How about down here?'

'Fine.'

She gripped the blouse below her right breast, and punched a hole in it. Holding the knife in her teeth, she inserted both forefingers into the opening and pulled. The cloth burst open. The tear shot up her front, the taut fabric parting over the mound of her breast. 'Oh shit,' she said, gazing down at the black protruding cup of her bra. 'Now what'll I do? I can't go to the party like this.'

'You could.'

'Aleshia's mom'll be there. *And* Miss Bennett. Besides, all the guys would gawk and act like jerks. I'd better go back and change.'

'What'll your parents say?'

'Oh geez. I'll try to sneak in...'

'I have an idea. Let's trade.'

'Thanks, but I don't think my blouse will fit you.'

'I can just wear the jacket,' he said, taking it off. Looking up and down the block, he saw nobody except a group of distant trick-or-treaters. He started to unbutton his shirt.

'I can't take your shirt.'

'Just put it on over yours.'

'You'll freeze.'

Shivering, he handed his shirt to Beth. He put on his

sports jacket. Its lining felt cool and slick against his skin. With shaking hands, he fastened the two front buttons.

Beth put on his shirt. 'Now we *really* look weird.'

'The weirder, the better.'

As they walked along, Eric rubbed burnt cork onto his neck and chest. Then he added Vampire Blood, squirting it onto his skin and letting it dribble.

'Want some more?' he asked.

'No thanks.'

He put it away. 'You know how to walk?'

Beth shrugged. 'Let's see you do it.'

'Like this, sort of.' He waddled, arms stiff at his sides, his mouth hanging open, eyes wide and staring. 'And you moan. See, the idea is, we're the living dead and we want to eat everybody we see.'

'Yum yum.'

Side by side, they lurched across the road. As they moved slowly up the block, a group of trick-or-treaters left a dark porch and crossed the lawn to the sidewalk.

'Let's give 'em a scare,' Beth whispered.

Ahead of them, a small girl in a Wonder Woman costume stepped off the sidewalk and stared. A cowboy drew his revolver. He fired, yelling, '*Pow pow pow!*' as his hammer clanked down. Eric and Beth stalked forward. The cowboy jumped out of their way, but Darth Vader blocked the sidewalk.

'What're you supposed to be?' he demanded.

Beth groaned, and reached for him.

He backed away, stepping on the toe of a bunny behind him. The bunny shoved him, snapping 'Watch it!'

Darth Vader ignored him. 'I'm not scared of you creeps.'

In a low voice, Eric muttered, 'We're gonna eat you.'

'Oh yeah? You and who else?'

'Me,' said Beth. 'Yum yum.'

'Go fuck yourselves,' he blurted, and dashed around them. He ran into Wonder Woman, knocking her to the grass. Eric stepped toward the girl, wanting to help her, but she squealed in terror and scrambled to her feet and ran away.

Eric returned to Beth.

She shrugged. 'Guess that didn't work out too well.'

'Creepy kid.'

When they met trick-or-treaters at the corner, they walked normally and had no trouble. They crossed the street. Ahead of them, a car stopped. Its rear doors opened and two figures climbed out. The car moved on.

'They must be for the party,' Beth said.

'Is that Aleshia's house?'

'Yeah. Come on, let's go into our routine.'

Stiff-armed and moaning, they shambled up the sidewalk.

31

'I don't know about this.'

'What's to know, jack-off? It's Halloween! We're just a couple of trick-or-treaters.' Nate drove slowly past Miss Bennett's house. At the end of the block, he pulled to the curb.

'Maybe we oughtta forget about it,' Bill said.

Nate shut off the headlights. 'Hey, what's the point in knowing where she lives if we're not gonna pay a visit? Come on.' Nate climbed out of the car.

Bill hesitated, then swung open the passenger door. As he climbed out, the cold wind hit him and he wished he'd dressed more warmly. He might, at least, have worn shoes and socks instead of sandals.

Nate opened the trunk and took off his jacket. He turned to Bill, arms out. 'How do I look?'

'Cold.'

'I can take it.'

Like Bill, he wore sandals, jeans cut off raggedly at the knees, and a sheath knife on his rope belt. While Bill wore a striped T-shirt that gave him some protection against the weather, Nate wore only an open leather vest.

'Catch this,' he said. He spread the flaps of his vest,

195

and Bill saw a rough drawing of a skull and crossbones on Nate's chest.

'Didn't know you're an artist.'

'I'm a man of many talents.' He flipped a black patch down, covering his left eye. Then he reached into the trunk and took out two grocery bags. 'For our goodies,' he said, handing one to Bill.

Side by side, they headed for Miss Bennett's house. Her front porch light was on. A jack-o'-lantern grinned at them through her picture window.

'Now don't do anything dumb,' Bill warned.

'Dumb? Me?'

'We'll just ring her doorbell, and trick-or-treat, and that's all.'

'Sure.'

'I mean it.' Bill adjusted the red bandanna tied around his head. He touched the big, hooped earring that hung from his right ear, and wondered if he should pluck it off; he didn't want to look silly.

'What're you waiting for?' Nate asked.

'Do I look okay?'

'You look gorgeous. The baddest buccaneer that ever sailed the Seven Seas.'

Bill reached toward the doorbell.

''Cept your tool's out.'

Bill pressed the button. Then, though he knew Nate was joking, he touched his fly. He found it safely zipped.

'Had you worried.'

'Sure.'

The door opened.

Miss Bennett smiled out at them. Her face was smeared with soot. She wore a shapeless felt hat, a bandanna around her neck, a shirt of red flannel, and baggy brown pants held up by suspenders. A polka-dot patch adorned one knee of her trousers.

'Trick-or-treat,' said Bill and Nate.

'What have we here? A pirate and an exhibitionist?'

Nate made a crooked smile. 'Guess you're a tramp.'

She laughed. '*Touché*! A hit, a palpable hit. Come on in out of the cold. Do you like cider?'

'Sure,' Bill said.

They stepped into the house. Miss Bennett closed the door. As she turned away, Nate nudged Bill with his elbow and winked his uncovered eye.

'You boys must be freezing,' she said.

'We're tough,' said Nate.

They entered the living room. 'Have a seat. I've got hot cider on the stove. I'll be back in a jiff.'

Bill sat on the sofa, and watched her walk away. A polka-dot patch covered the seat of her pants. Nate winked again, and dropped into a stuffed chair near the corner. 'Still think this was a lousy idea?'

Bill shook his head, grinning.

'Got you to first base. Imagination and guts, that's all it takes.'

A hand reached from behind the chair and clutched Nate's shoulder. With a yelp, he leaped to his feet. As he whirled around, a black-clad Frankenstein monster rose into view. Nate backed away. 'Very funny,' he told the monster. 'You're a real barrel of yucks.'

It slowly stepped from behind the chair. Arms out, it lurched toward Nate.

Bill saw Miss Bennett in the kitchen doorway, shaking as she tried to hold in her laughter.

Nate continued to back away from the monster. 'Okay! A joke's a joke. Now knock it off!'

It kept coming.

'Damn!' He put up his fists. 'One more step, shit-head!'

'That's enough,' Miss Bennett said in a calm voice.

The monster's huge, misshapen head turned toward her.

'Sit down and be good,' she said.

It lowered its arms. It turned away and lumbered back to the chair where Nate had been sitting. With a quiet grunt, it sat down. It folded its hands and crossed its legs.

'Sorry if he scared you,' Miss Bennett said, coming in with two mugs of cider.

Nate smirked and snorted. He sat on the sofa beside Bill.

'Who are you?' Bill asked the monster.

The monster sat motionless, and said nothing.

'Who is it, Miss Bennett?'

'My friend, the Wretch.'

'Makes *me* want to retch,' Nate muttered.

'He's quite harmless, normally.' Miss Bennett set down the mugs on the coffee table.

Bill thanked her, and picked one up. Pushing a cinnamon stick aside, he took a sip. 'That's good.'

'It'll warm your bones,' she said. She crossed the room, and sat down on the lap of the Wretch. 'So, what're you fellows up to?'

'We're gonna pillage the town,' Nate said.

'Actually, we're going to a Halloween party, but that's not till later.'

'Same with us.'

'We're not keeping you, are we?'

'No. There's no rush.'

'You heading over to the Sherwood place?' Nate asked.

'One of my students is having a few people over.' She slapped one of the monster's hands as it slid up her thigh. 'There's a party at the Sherwood...?' The doorbell interrupted her. 'Excuse me,' she said. She pushed the Wretch's hand off her leg, and went to the door.

Bill heard her open it. A chorus of children's voices called out, 'Trick-or-treat.'

Across the room, the monster stood. It began walking slowly toward Nate.

'Okay, Wretch, knock it off.'

It raised its arms.

Nate jumped to his feet. 'Okay, asshole.'

The monster reached out for him.

Nate kicked. His foot shot toward the crotch, but a quick hand blocked his blow, gripped Nate's ankle and threw him backwards. He hit the floor, his head barely missing the coffee table.

Bill sprang to his feet, ready to fight, but the monster held up its hand. 'I've got no quarrel with you,' said a voice muffled by the mask.

'Lay off Nate.'

'I'm done with him.' The monster's hands fumbled with its mask then pulled it off.

Mr Carlson, the school librarian, frowned down at Nate. 'That was for yesterday, Houlder, for knocking her into the bushes.'

'You cocksucker,' Nate muttered. 'I'm gonna sue your ass.'

'I believe this falls into the category of self-defense.'

'What's going on here?' Miss Bennett asked, frowning as she entered the room.

'Houlder was just leaving.'

'Damn it, Nick!'

'Sorry,' he said. 'But Houlder had it coming.'

'An eye for an eye never solved anything.'

'It helps, believe me.'

'That's right, man,' Nate said as he got to his feet. 'You just remember that. 'Cause you're gonna pay.' He flipped open his vest and tapped the skull-and-crossbones drawn on his chest. 'See this? You're gonna look worse by the time I'm done. Count on it.'

'You scare me, Houlder.'

Nate's hand darted to the hilt of his knife. He unsnapped the sheath.

Bill grabbed his wrist. 'Come on, Nate. Let's get out of here.'

He held on until Nate's arm relaxed.

'Yeah, okay. Let's go.'

Miss Bennett hurried ahead of them, and opened the door.

'Sorry about this,' Bill told her. 'But your friend did start it. Nate was just sitting there.'

She nodded and said nothing.

'Carlson started it,' Nate said, 'but I'm gonna finish it.' He stopped at the door and looked back at the black-clad man. 'You hear that, Carlson? I'm gonna finish it. An eye for an eye.'

'Just try it, Houlder.'

Bill tugged Nate's sleeve. 'Come on.'

They stepped outside, and Miss Bennett shut the door.

32

'So then Doons accused *me* of being Houlder's girl-friend.'

'Doons is a jerk,' Eric said.

'I hate him.'

'Me too.' He finished his plastic glass of punch, and saw that Beth was nearly done. 'You want some more?'

'Yeah. Good, isn't it?'

'Yeah.' He took her glass. I'll be right back.' She smiled, and Eric left her. He made his way across the living room, looking for gaps through the frantic dancers and watching the girls. They paid no attention to him as he weaved among them. Most had vacant looks in their eyes as if entranced by the loud music and the motions of their own jerking bodies.

Aleshia wore pink tights and a white tutu. Her shoulders were bare. A pearl choker hung at her throat, and she wore a tiara in her hair. Eric had never seen her look so beautiful. If only he were more like Eddie Ryker ... He watched Eddie dance. The tall, handsome boy wore no real costume – just a football jersey and jeans. He had a complacent smile. His eyes were on the ceiling – not even *looking* at her!

Eric bumped into someone.

'Jesus, Prince!' Mark Bailey scowled at him from under his helmet liner.

'Sorry sir,' Eric said, and snapped a salute.

'Creep,' muttered Mark's partner.

Eric turned to her. Sue Diamond, the head cheerleader. She, too, was apparently dressed as a soldier. She wore a tiger-striped field hat, a drab olive jumpsuit, and a canteen on a web belt. Her jumpsuit was unzipped almost to her belly, showing a long V of bare skin and no trace of bra.

'Fuck off,' she said.

Eric hurried past, then looked back, wondering what would show if she bent down. She didn't bend down. Instead, she gave him the finger.

He finally reached the refreshment table. He stood in line behind a clown and a vampire. Nobody spoke to him. He waited, watching Elmer Cantwell dip punch from the cut-glass bowl for the vampire.

Elmer seemed to be dressed as the hunchback of Notre Dame. With his squat figure and bulgy eyes, he looked right for the role.

'Is that Aleshia's father?' Eric had asked when he first saw Elmer.

'No,' Beth told him. 'Her dad's never home. That's Elmer Cantwell.'

'What's he doing here?'

'He's a friend of Aleshia's mom. Ugly, isn't he?'

'Sort of.'

'Women are supposed to be crazy about him. I can't see it, though, can you?'

Eric had shaken his head.

'He must have something going for him, 'cause it sure isn't his looks.'

'Maybe he's rich.'

'Maybe.'

The vampire and clown were gone, and Eric looked across the table at the man. He saw the eyes lower to his bare chest, and stare. He fought an urge to pull his jacket shut.

'Two punches, please.'

Elmer grinned, showing his crooked upper teeth, and reached for the empty glasses. Eric held them out. The man's fingers stroked his hands. He squirmed, wishing Aleshia's mother was still at the punch bowl instead of this man.

Elmer took the glasses. He set them down, dipped into the punch bowl, and filled them with the frothy red liquid.

'I've seen you at the library, Eric,' he said in a whispery voice.

'You have?'

'Many times.'

'Where?'

'The public library.'

'Oh.'

'You have such lovely skin. A shame to hide it under such filth.'

'Oh.' He felt as if worms were crawling on his back. 'Thanks for the punch,' he said. He picked up the two glasses and hurried away. This time, passing through the dancers, he didn't even notice those around him. He found Beth still standing in the corner. Mary Lou, one of the cheerleaders, was with her.

'Hi Eric,' Mary Lou said.

She was a slim redhead, dressed as a nurse.

'Hi.'

'Are you okay?' Beth asked.

'Sure.' He handed a glass to her.

'You look sick.'

'I'm the living dead.'

'What happened?'

He shrugged. 'Oh, that guy Elmer.'

'What'd he do?' Mary Lou asked.

'He's just a creep.'

'Do you know what he said to John? You know John? He's Dracula. He was in front of you. Did you hear what that crazy guy said to him?'

Eric shook his head.

'Get this.' Mary Lou glanced from Beth to Eric, her eyes bright and eager. 'He said, "You can suck me anytime, Count."'

'Good Christ,' Beth muttered.

'Gross, huh?'

'Is he ... gay?' Beth asked.

'God, I guess so. But you know, he's supposed to be a real lady-killer.'

'Maybe he likes both,' Eric said.

Beth shook her head. 'I don't see why anybody'd be interested in *him*.'

'Haven't you heard? He's...' Mary Lou glanced at Eric, then back to Beth. 'Well ... They say he's got an absolutely enormous *thing*.'

'Yuck,' Beth said.

'It's supposed to be – you know – gigantuous.'

'Do you think he and Aleshia's mom...?'

'Why else would he be here?'

'Boy,' Beth muttered. She wrinkled her nose as if disgusted.

Mary Lou turned to Eric. 'So look, what'd he say to you?'

'He said I've got nice skin.'

'Oh gross.'

As she sipped her punch, Beth's eyes lowered to Eric's chest, and lingered there. 'He's right,' she finally said.

Laughter burst from Mary Lou. 'You're a nut!' she gasped. 'God what a nut!'

Beth set down her drink. Her mouth dropped open, her head tilted to one side, and she gazed at Mary Lou with wide, vacant eyes. Moaning, she raised her arms. She reached for the girl's throat.

'Hey!' Giggling, Mary Lou backed away.

'Gonna eat you,' Beth mumbled. 'Yum yum.'

Eric started to shamble alongside Beth. 'Gonna eat you.'

Mary Lou backed into John the vampire. She squealed as he threw his arms around her and nibbled the side of her neck.

'Wanta get Aleshia?' Eric asked.

Beth nodded.

They moved slowly across the room, moaning, bumping into dancers who ignored them or laughed or pushed them away. Then Aleshia was in front of them. Her head was back, her eyes half-shut and dreamy as she shrugged and flung her arms and twirled. They staggered past Eddie Ryker. He kept on dancing as if they were invisible.

'Gonna eat you,' Beth mumbled.

Aleshia paid no attention.

Eric saw specks of sweat on her upper lip, but her shoulders and chest looked dry. The tops of her breasts showed above her bodice. One hard downward pull would free them...

And every guy in the room would jump on Eric.

Beth grabbed Aleshia's arm.

'Hey!'

'Gonna eat you,' Beth said.

'Oh yeah?' Aleshia pulled free, grinning. 'Nobody eats me but Eddie.'

Beth gasped and burst into laughter.

With a harsh laugh, Aleshia resumed her dance.

Eric watched, sick with disappointment. Why hadn't he grabbed her? At least her arm, like Beth?

Shit!

He'd missed his chance. He'd chickened out.

'Want to dance?' Beth asked.

'I guess.'

33

'It's stopping,' Bill said.

Nate slowed down.

A block in front of them, the car containing Carlson and Miss Bennett backed into a space along the curb.

'That's gotta be the place,' Nate said.

'Yeah.' The house was bright, its porch light on, a green spotlight on the front lawn illuminating a stiff-armed motionless figure.

'Keep an eye on 'em,' Nate said.

Bill watched Carlson and Miss Bennett climb from the car. They turned toward the lighted house and strolled up its walkway. The solitary figure didn't move. A scarecrow, Bill realized as they drove slowly closer.

He saw a grinning jack-o'-lantern in the picture window. Beyond it, people in costumes were standing around, some dancing. 'Kids,' he said.

'And to think we weren't invited. What kind of asshole has a party and doesn't invite us?'

The screen door opened. Carlson and Miss Bennett entered.

'Pisses me off. What do they think we are, lepers? You got leprosy, dingus?'

'Nope.'

'Me either. The fuck-heads.'

At the end of the block, he turned the corner and parked.

'What're you doing?'

'What does it look like?'

'We're not going in.'

'Hey, we're trick-or-treaters. We'll just go up to the door and see what develops.'

'Bullshit. You want to get in there and wipe out Carlson.'

With a wink, Nate flipped the black patch down. 'Fuckin'-A right. We bad dudes, man. Pirates. Nobody pushes us around. We do the pushing.' He threw open the car door and leaped out. Running up the street, he cried out, 'Rape, plunder, pillage! Ho ho ho and a bottle of rum!'

Bill ran after him. 'Wait up!'

'Fuck you, slowpoke.'

'Hey you kids!' yelled a woman.

Bill spotted her on the sidewalk with half a dozen children.

'Eat it, lady!' Nate called back as he cut across the corner lot.

She was still ahead of Bill. 'You creeps oughtta be locked up!'

'Up your ass!' Bill yelled.

'Right on!' Nate shouted from a distance.

Bill stayed on the road until he passed the woman, then he dashed over the sidewalk and across the corner yard. Nate, just ahead, jumped up and down waiting for him.

'Come on, dipstick!'

Side by side, they ran down the block.

'Rape pillage plunder!' Nate shouted.

Rock music blared from the house ahead. *'I'm dying to be your woman, I 'm dying to be your guy, we're dying to be red-hot lovers – under the sunbeam sky.'* Nate sprinted toward the scarecrow. Its head was a painted grocery bag. *'Under the sunbeam sky sky sky.'*

'Yeeyah!' He crashed into it. The post snapped, and he drove the scarecrow to the ground. It came apart at the waist. Balls of wadded newspaper spilled out of its shirt and pants.

'Dying to be lovers, dying to get high, dying to be your wonder-waker under the red-hot sky.'

Rolling, he scrambled to his feet and rushed the door. The main door stood open.

'Nate!'

'Rape pillage plunder!'

'Don't!'

He flung open the screen door. A woman in an evening gown blocked his way. He smashed her aside.

Bill hesitated. He didn't want to follow Nate inside, wanted no part of the fight and destruction sure to come.

Eric was dancing with Beth, watching her and trying to imitate her moves when he saw a pirate plow into Mrs Barnes. The woman yelped and stumbled backwards. She hit the wall hard.

'I'm dying to go down with you, I'm dying to feel your skin.'

'Rape pillage plunder!' the pirate yelled.

Nate Houlder!

'*We're dying to be red-hot lovers – doing the sunbeam sin.*'

Nate charged across the room, smashing his way through startled dancers.

'Stop him!' someone shouted.

'Get him!'

Eddie Ryker reached out, as Nate rushed by, and grabbed his shoulder. Nate whirled and slammed a fist into Ryker's nose. Jerking free, he lunged at the Frankenstein monster – Mr Carlson – who'd come in with Miss Bennett only a minute ago. Carlson landed a punch on his chin, but it didn't stop him. He threw himself against the man, grappled with him, drove a knee up into his groin. Carlson cried out and fell. Nate scurried over him. Reached the refreshment table. Elmer backed away, and Nate lifted the punch bowl.

'No!' Miss Bennett yelled.

He lurched toward Carlson, stumbled, and emptied the punch onto him. The red flood washed over his head and back, splashed off him and spattered those nearby.

Miss Bennett wrenched the empty bowl away from Nate. 'You idiot!' she snapped. 'You stupid goddamned idiot!'

'My *carpet*!' shrieked Mrs Barnes.

'Get him!' cried Aleshia. 'Everybody get him!'

Three of the guys from the football team – Mark Bailey the soldier, John the vampire, and an Indian – hit him at the same time. He went down in a pile of bodies.

'Go help,' Beth said, nudging Eric.

'They don't want me.'

'Go on. They'll think you're chicken.'

'Well...' He left Beth. By the time he reached the group, six boys were on Nate. Aleshia stood over them, giving directions. Her face was red and she was breathing hard.

'His leg,' she gasped. 'Get his other leg.'

Eric crouched and grabbed Nate's left ankle – the only visible part of his body.

'Okay, pick him up. Pick him up.'

'Let's call the cops,' said John.

'No. I've got a better idea. Get him outside.'

John and a cowboy climbed off Nate. The others lifted him.

'My carpet,' muttered Mrs Barnes.

'He'll pay for it,' said Elmer.

Eric walked backwards, still holding Nate's ankle. The foot was bare. Nate was panting, sobbing. His eyepatch hung around his neck. Blood trickled from his nostrils. The right side of his face was red and swollen. His chest bled from a dozen fingernail scratches.

'What're we gonna do with him?' Ryker asked.

'Get him outside,' Aleshia said again.

'I think the police should be notified,' Miss Bennett said as she walked behind the group.

'We'll take care of him.'

'He's been hurt enough.'

'We won't hurt him,' said Aleshia.

Somebody held open the screen door. They carried Nate outside, and down the porch steps.

'Okay,' Aleshia said. 'Strip him.'

'Yeah!' said the cowboy.

'All *right*!' said the Indian.

'Serve the bastard right,' said Ryker.

'Kids!' snapped Miss Bennett. 'I don't think this is the right way to...'

A wild cry of rage stopped her voice.

Eric dropped Nate's foot as he saw a pirate leap from behind a nearby bush.

'Bill!' Miss Bennett shouted.

The pirate glanced at her, but didn't stop. He dived onto the backs of three boys, throwing them forward across Nate's body, smashing them into those on the other side. A couple stumbled backwards and stayed on their feet, but the rest fell in a tangled mass.

'Boys!' Miss Bennett yelled. 'Boys, stop it!'

'Get him!' Aleshia shouted, jumping up and down.

Ryker and Bailey, the ones still standing, went for Bill. They grabbed his arms and shoulders, trying to drag him off the others.

Nate, no longer held by anyone, rolled over. He got to his hands and knees. He started to crawl.

'Boys!'

'Oh no you don't,' said Beth. She leaped onto Nate's back, driving him to the ground. She straddled him. She shoved his shoulders, trying to keep him down, but he rolled onto his back and snarled up at her.

'You,' he muttered. His hands flailed. Beth tried to catch them, but they clutched her breasts, squeezed and twisted. She shrieked.

Her cry of pain tore at Eric. He rushed forward and kicked. The toe of his sneaker caught Nate on the cheek. Nate cried out and grabbed his face.

He pulled Beth to her feet. She was crying softly. 'Are you okay?'

She shook her head, and stepped into Eric's arms. He held her. She felt soft and warm.

Bill lay on the ground, battered, keeping his eyes shut. If they realized he was conscious, they might start in again. Through the ringing in his ears, he heard voices.

Aleshia. 'Okay, get their clothes off.'

Miss Bennett. 'I'm calling the police.'

'No, let's go ahead and let them, Karen.' Who was that? Carlson, probably. The Wretch. 'It's harmless.'

'It's not harmless, its disgusting and degrading.'

'And appropriate. Christ, look what Houlder did to me. Not to mention the carpet.'

'Let's not spoil the fun,' said a quiet, whispery voice.

'Do what you want with them.' The unfamiliar voice of a woman. 'As far as I'm concerned, you can boil them in oil.'

'Let's take a vote,' Aleshia said. 'All in favor of stripping the bastards?'

Bill heard a chorus of *ayes* and *yeahs*.

'Opposed?'

'You're all crazy,' Miss Bennett said.

'The ayes have it.'

Hands began to tug Bill's T-shirt.

'I'm calling the police.'

'Not from my house. The party's over. If you're so eager to help these ruffians, go home and call.'

'Mrs Barnes, I don't think . . .'

'Maybe we should leave,' Carlson said.

'Yes. Maybe we should.'

His shirt was off. He felt the cold, wet grass under his back.

'Geez, look at this knife.'

'Take it,' Aleshia said. 'Take everything.'

He felt hands on his rope belt, on the button of his jeans. The zipper slid down. He raised his head, opened his eyes, and the soldier crouching near his head smashed him in the face with a helmet liner.

His jeans were jerked down his legs.

'What about his shorts?'

'Take 'em. Take everything.'

Someone pulled his underpants off.

'All *right*!' Aleshia cried.

He heard giggles from several girls.

'Tiny little crittur,' said a boy.

'Nothing to brag about, is it?'

'Probably couldn't get it up if he had to.'

'You ever see one of these, Mary Lou?'

'Up yours.'

'Hey, get a load of this one.'

'I always knew Houlder was an eunuch.'

Laughter and giggles.

'Okay,' said Aleshia. 'Let's go back in and boogie.'

'Right!'

'No way. The party's over.'

'*Mom!*'

'You heard me.'

'But we only started!'

'It's over.'

'There's a party at the Sherwood house,' said a new voice. Who was that? Oh yeah. Prince. That little fart, Eric Prince. 'Why don't we all go over there?'

'Yeah!'

'Right! I got an invitation.'

'Who's giving the party?'

'Who knows?'

'Who cares!'

'Let's go!'

'All *right*!'

'What'll we do with these guys?'

'Leave 'em.'

'Yeah. But let's take their clothes. If they want 'em back, they'll have to come to the party.'

'Yeah, dressed as skinny-dippers.'

'Streakers.'

'A prick and an asshole.'

Bill heard laughter, and finally silence. Then a familiar voice said, 'We been screwed, dingus.'

'Yeah,' he muttered.

'We gonna let 'em away with it?'

34

'Looks like we're the first here,' Doons said. He slowed, made a U-turn, and parked in front of the Sherwood house.

'Oh, I don't know,' Marjorie said.

'You see any other cars? How many? Nine? Ten?'

'Lay off her, Phil.'

'When I need your advice, I'll ask for it.'

'Tough guy,' Thelma said.

'Damn right.'

'Let's not argue,' said Marjorie. 'This is Halloween. We're supposed to have fun.'

Thelma snorted. 'I just hope there're some decent men at this thing.'

'Oh, I'm sure there will. It'll be fun. I've always wanted to see inside the old place, haven't you?'

'Hardly.'

Doons climbed out of the car, and opened its rear door. Thelma scooted out first, reaching up a hand for assistance. He gave her a pull.

'What a dear,' she said.

'I know it.' He helped Marjorie out. 'Will that be all ladies?'

'Oh Phillip.'

'He's pissed 'cause he had to sit alone.'

'I should've come dressed as a chauffeur.'

'You look fine, darling.'

'I feel like an ass.' He jammed his hands into the pockets of his bib overalls. Marjorie had rushed out to buy them after he phoned about the party. She'd bought similar overalls for herself and Thelma.

Thank God, Doons thought, she couldn't find anyplace selling straw hats.

Three fuckin' hayseeds.

'You *have* to dress up,' Marjorie had insisted. 'It's a costume party.'

'The place looks deserted,' Thelma said, interrupting his thoughts.

'That's what I said.'

They started across the front yard, walking through its high weeds.

'You know what?' Thelma asked. Her voice was quiet and missing its usual sarcasm. 'I saw Dexter go in this place the other night.'

Marjorie gaped. 'Really?'

'Yeah. The night he was killed, in fact.'

'Oh my goodness!'

Doons snorted. 'How'd you happen to see that? Or shouldn't I ask?'

Thelma ignored him. 'I saw him go in the back door. And he didn't come out.'

Doons stopped near the veranda. He turned to Thelma. 'What are you, trying to scare us?'

'I just wanted to mention it.'

'You don't think...' Marjorie started.

'I don't know,' said Thelma. 'I told that cop about it,

and he seemed awfully interested. He was so interested, in fact, that he didn't bother to pull me in.'

Doons blew air through his gritted teeth. 'Jesus Christ, Thelma, what're we doing here?'

'Going to a party.'

In a calm voice, Marjorie added, 'You're the one who suggested it, Phil.'

'Well Jeezus, nobody told me this is where Boyanski got his ticket cancelled.'

'Don't worry about it,' Thelma said. 'It probably didn't happen here, anyway. Let's go in and have a good time.'

'Sure.' Doons didn't move.

With a smirk, Thelma hooked her thumbs into her overall pockets and climbed the front steps.

'This is crazy,' Doons said.

'Don't be a spoilsport,' Marjorie said. She took Doons's hand. Together, they followed Thelma up the steps to the front door.

'You planning to make me open it?' Thelma asked.

He reached for the knob. As his fingers curved around it, the door flew open. He jumped with alarm. Thelma gasped. Marjorie yelped and clutched his arm.

Inside stood a woman dressed in a long white gown. She held a lighted candle. Her face was in shadows. 'Phil?' she asked.

He managed not to sigh with relief as he recognized the voice. 'Barbara?'

'Boy, am I glad to see you. This place was giving me the willies.'

'Barbara, you've met my wife Marjorie. This is her sister, Thelma. Thelma, this is Barbara Major, one of the teachers from school.'

'Hello,' Thelma said.

'Nice to meet you. Come on in.'

'Anybody else here yet?' Doons asked as he stepped inside.

'See for yourself.'

The women entered and he shut the door. The foyer was dark except for Barbara's candle. They walked slowly over the hardwood floor, and passed through the entryway to the living room.

'Jesus Christ,' Doons muttered.

The candlelit room was deserted except for three gorillas hanging by their arms from wrought-iron window grates.

'Are they real?' Marjorie whispered.

'They're costumes,' said Barbara.

'Anyone in them?' Thelma asked,

Barbara shrugged. 'I haven't gone close enough to find out. They don't move, though. I think they're just stuffed. They sure give me the willies, though. I was about to leave when you guys came along.'

'Let's have a look,' Doons said.

'You look,' said Thelma. 'I'm getting a drink.' She started across the room toward a table at the far end.

'Not a bad idea.' Doons followed her, flanked by Marjorie and Barbara. He realized that he was walking strangely, rolling from heel to toe in an effort to quiet his footfalls. His stomach muscles felt tight. He kept his eyes on the gorillas.

They hung several yards apart along the left-hand wall, each in front of a different window. Their wrists seemed to be bound to the upper crossbars, suspending them well above the floor. Doons could stand on a chair, he decided, and pull off the headgear to see who – if anyone – was inside. But there were no chairs in the room. Only the table.

Thelma was already there. Doons flinched at the sudden noise she made dumping a handful of ice cubes into a plastic glass. 'Gilby's Vodka,' she announced. 'Whoever's throwing this bash has decent taste.'

'Eric Prince,' Barbara said.

'His mother must've bought the booze,' Doons said.

'Where *is* everyone?' Marjorie asked.

As Doons pulled three glasses from the stack, Barbara said, 'Eric told me he'd invited a whole bunch of people.'

'And we're the only ones dumb enough to come.' Doons quietly filled the glasses with ice from a plastic bag.

'It's early yet,' said Thelma.

Marjorie frowned. 'You'd think the host, at least, would be here.'

'You're right.' Doons turned around, eyeing each of the gorillas. 'He's probably in one of those monkey suits. Hey Eric!' he called out. No answer came. None of the gorillas moved. 'Bet he is.'

'Wouldn't surprise me,' Barbara whispered. 'He's a spooky little kid.'

'What'll you have?'

'Bourbon and Seven.'

He poured Barbara's drink. 'How about you, honey?'

'Scotch and soda.'

He made it for her, and poured scotch for himself. He sipped it, and immediately felt more relaxed. Comforting, he thought, to have a familiar drink in your

221

hand. 'Well, shall we have a look at our three silent friends?'

'Help yourself,' said Thelma. 'I'm staying here at the comfort station.'

A dozen lighted candles stood on the floor along the wall. Doons crouched over one near the center gorilla. It clung to the floor with dripped wax. He pulled it free, and stood. Holding it high, he studied the gorilla's face. He was too low to see into the sunken eye-holes.

'Hello?' he asked.

No answer.

'Anybody home? Eric?' He pressed the thick, black fur of its leg. 'Feels like someone's in there.' He jabbed his fingers against it. 'Yoo-hooo. Hello in there. Speak now or forever hold your peace.'

Marjorie took a step backward. 'Maybe we should leave it alone.'

'Bullshit.' Doons reached up to the gorilla's groin and goosed it.

'Phil!'

Barbara laughed.

The gorilla didn't move.

Doons shrugged and took a sip of scotch. 'Hell with it,' he muttered. 'Let's have a look at . . .'

A blast of rock music hit his ears. He swung around and saw Thelma on her knees beneath the table. The volume lowered. She got up and looked around. 'Radio,' she explained. She stepped aside and Doons saw a radio the size of a briefcase under the table. 'Now all we need are a couple of men. How about the monkeys?' Holding her drink high, she pursed her lips and danced toward the nearest gorilla.

Doons shook his head. 'You've always had a fondness for big apes.'

She made a loud, sucking kiss in his direction and continued to dance toward the gorilla at the last window. Doons watched. She looked ridiculous – vaguely repellent – shaking her shoulders and ass.

'What a sight,' he muttered.

Barbara smiled at him, as if sharing his opinion. For the first time tonight, he looked closely at her. She wore a red corsage above one breast. Her straps were red velvet, the rest of her dress white.

'Cinderella?' Doons asked.

'This is my old prom dress. Thought I'd come disguised as a kid.'

'You look beautiful,' Marjorie said.

'Nice,' Doons agreed. If enough people would show up, he planned to get her alone in one of the upstairs rooms. They'd do it on the floor or up against a wall. He'd ruck up her dress. She wouldn't have underwear on – she never did. It'd make the damned party worth the bother.

'Get on down,' Thelma said, tugging the leg of the far gorilla. 'Come on, hon. Get on down and boogie.'

It dropped from the window bars. Its feet thudded the floor. It stood in front of Thelma, crouching, arms out. A short length of rope hung from each wrist.

'Well well!' she said. She downed the rest of her vodka, tossed the glass over her shoulder, and stepped into the arms of the gorilla.

It lifted Thelma off her feet.

'My kind of guy!' she announced.

It carried her down the center of the room. She hung on, one arm hooked around the back of its neck, and waved as she passed Doons.

'Phil!' Marjorie whispered.

He looked at her and shrugged.

'Find out who it is.'

He didn't want to. But he couldn't let himself look like a coward in front of Barbara. 'Hey you,' he called.

The gorilla stopped. It stood near the opening to the foyer. All of Thelma but her dangling legs was blocked by the gorilla's broad, hairy back.

'Who are you?' Doons demanded.

'He's my gorgeous hunk,' said Thelma. 'Bug off.' In a softer voice, she said, 'Come on, hon. Take me to your tree. Bet you've got a banana for me, huh?'

The gorilla carried her from the room.

Doons heard her husky laughter in the foyer.

'Phil!'

'She's got what she wants. Why fight it?'

Marjorie hissed through her nose. '*I'm* seeing where they go.'

'Oh, for . . .' He stopped himself. If Marjorie followed the two, he would have a few minutes alone with Barbara. 'Go ahead, if you want.'

She hurried on tiptoes toward the front of the room, back hunched, arms flapping like a crazed tightrope artist about to fall.

Doons winked at Barbara. She took a small step closer.

Marjorie stopped at the wall and peered around it.

Barbara patted Doons's rump.

Marjorie looked back. She pointed upward.

'They're going upstairs?'

She nodded.

'You gonna follow them?'

Shaking her head, she pointed at Doons.

'You want *me* to follow them?'

She nodded and waved him forward.

He turned to Barbara. 'Want to come along?'

'Sure.'

They walked over to Marjorie. 'You really want me to go upstairs?'

'I'm worried, Phil. Heaven only knows who might be inside that suit.' She turned her eyes to the two gorillas still suspended from the window bars. 'Or in those.'

'I guess we'd better all go up together. I'm warning you, though, Marjorie – Thelma's gonna be plenty pissed if we interrupt her in the middle of a good . . . an *intimate* moment.'

'We'll be quiet.'

Doons grinned at Barbara. 'My wife's a closet voyeur.'

'So am I.'

Doons led the way. He walked slowly up the stairs, lowering each foot with great care. In spite of his caution, every stair squeaked and groaned under his weight.

They were halfway to the top of the when the front door swung open. Doons gripped the bannister and looked down. Aleshia Barnes, dressed in tights and a tutu, stood in the doorway grinning at them.

'Trick-or-treat, everyone!'

Doons pressed a finger to his lips.

Eddie Ryker came in behind her, followed by a group

of kids in costume. 'Mr Doons?' Eddie asked. 'What's going on?'

'We just have to check on something. You kids go ahead and have fun.'

'Anything we can help you with?'

Doons pictured the whole bunch walking in on Thelma as she lay on the floor rutting with the gorilla. 'No,' he said. 'We'll take care of it. You all go ahead and start the party. We'll be down in a minute.'

35

Eric entered the house beside Beth, and saw the group on the stairway: Doons, Miss Major and a stranger. The unfamiliar woman wore bib overalls and a plaid shirt, like Doons. Probably his wife. Eric shook his head, astonished that the v.p. and teacher had both shown up. It was almost too good to be true.

'Where're they going?' he asked.

'Doing something upstairs,' said Eddie.

'*Doing* something?' asked John the vampire, wriggling his eyebrows.

At the top of the stairway, the group turned left and disappeared.

'Where'll we put the guys' clothes and stuff?' asked Mary Lou.

'We'll think of something,' said Aleshia. 'Hang onto them for now. Come on.'

They followed Aleshia into the living room. 'Holy shit,' she muttered.

'Wow,' said Beth.

Eric stared, gaping at the rows of candles on the floor along each wall, at the pair of shaggy gorillas suspended from the window bars, at the crudely painted drawings.

The drawings fascinated Eric. He saw a witch riding

her broomstick across the ceiling – the witch naked, the broomstick a rigid penis. On a wall stood a black-hooded headsman, his bloody ax held high. Farther down the wall, a group of naked women were gathered in a circle munching parts of a dismembered man.

'Eric walked along the wall, looking closely.

'Sick,' Beth muttered. 'Really sick.'

'Yeah.'

He took a few more steps and saw the red-painted Devil sodomizing a woman.

'My God,' Beth said. She turned away. 'Come on. Let's stay with the others.'

Ahead of them, the group had split up – half continuing toward the refreshment table, the other half veering to the left for a closer look at the gorillas.

'God, you don't think there's anyone in those things?' Sue Diamond squeezed the leg of the nearest one.

Mark Bailey pounded the leg with his helmet liner. 'Nobody alive,' he said, and laughed.

'Very amusing.'

'Looky here! Booze!'

'All right!'

'Better get some before Doons comes down.'

'Fuck Doons.'

'Thanks but no thanks.'

'*Look* at this! Scotch, bourbon, vodka, gin. Jesus H. Christ, we can all tie one on.'

'Man, I'd like to meet the guy that's throwing this party. I'd like to shake his hand.'

'I'd like to kiss him.'

'You don't know who the host is?' asked a whispery voice from the rear.

Whirling around, Eric saw Elmer Cantwell lurch through the entryway and hobble forward.

'It is I,' he said. 'Hop-Frog.'

'Hey, well, it's fantastic!'

'I'm pleased that you're pleased.'

'I thought you were the hunchback of Notre Dame.'

'Hop-Frog,' he said, scurrying toward them. 'Hop-Frog at your service.'

'You sure know how to throw a party.'

They walked slowly down the hall, Doons in the lead with his candle, the two women close behind him. So far, they'd passed two doors. Both had been locked. Doons had rapped quietly on each with no response.

'Should we try calling out?' Marjorie whispered.

'No,' Doons said. He came to the door with a splintery hole hacked into it. Crouching slightly, he peered into the gap. A face appeared. He yelped and jumped back, bumping into Marjorie. She grabbed his arm.

'Hey,' a voice whispered from behind the door.

Doons took a deep, shaky breath. 'Good Christ,' he said. 'You scared the...'

'You've gotta get us out of here.'

'What're you doing in there?'

'He nailed the door shut.'

'Who?'

'There's a maniac in the house.'

'Oh my goodness!' Marjorie gasped.

'I think he killed the real estate guy. Morley? This afternoon. He tried to get us. He has a gun.'

'You on the level?'

'Look, you've gotta help us get out of here.'

'This is a joke, right? A Halloween prank?'

'It's no prank, damn it. Look, somebody went by here a minute ago. A woman. I heard her laughing. Thought she might be with the killer, so I kept down.'

'That was Thelma.'

'She's with a guy?'

'A gorilla.'

'Shit! You may think this is funny, pal, but...'

'A guy in a gorilla suit.'

'You know him?'

'Haven't seen his face. He was here when we arrived.'

'Oh Christ. Have you got a weapon?'

Doons shook his head.

'You'd better take this.'

'No!' cried a woman behind the door. 'It's all we've got.'

'It's okay, honey.'

'Harold!'

'We'll be all right,' he told her. Then a metal object was thrust through the hole in the door. A hatchet head. 'Take it,' he said, pushing the hatchet out.

Doons took it.

The face of the man reappeared. 'That's all the protection we had, mister. We're counting on you.'

Doons nodded.

'Go get the bastard.'

'Maybe we'd better get you out, first, and...'

'It'd take too long. If you want to save that lady's skin...'

'Yeah. Yeah, you're right.' Doons swung around. 'One of you gals go for the boys. Get 'em up here quick.'

'I'm staying with you,' said Marjorie.

'I'll go.'

Barbara raced up the hall.

'Excuse me,' Eric said. 'I need to find a bathroom. I'll be right back.'

Nodding, Beth raised a glass of bourbon to her lips. She tasted it and shivered.

Elmer hobbled in front of Eric. 'Enjoying the festivities?'

'Yeah.' Eric kept walking.

'The fun has barely begun.' He reached for Eric's arm.

Eric sidestepped. 'Don't touch me.'

'It's my party. I touch whomever I please.'

'It's not your party, you liar. It's *my* party. *Mine!* And I didn't invite you.'

Elmer chuckled and rolled his eyes. 'My mistake.'

'Damn right.' Eric shoved him aside, and hurried by.

He left the living room.

Miss Major came running down the stairs. 'Quick! Get all the guys! We need help!'

'Fuck you,' he said.

'Eric!'

He stepped to the front door, and removed a padlock from his pants pocket.

'Eric! What're you doing!'

The latch was where he'd been told it would be, where he'd seen it as he entered. He flipped it over the metal hoop on the doorframe, and snapped the padlock into place.

'Eric!'

'Nobody leaves.'

Miss Major gazed at him, her eyes wide, her mouth

231

hanging open. Then she ran into the living room. 'Help!' she cried out. 'Everyone! Upstairs!'

Doons blew out his candle and slid it into a pocket of his overalls. The hatchet was slippery in his wet hand. He reached for the doorknob, and slowly turned it.

This door was not locked.

He suddenly felt as if he would lose control of his bowels. He clamped his buttocks together and clenched his sphincter. He took a deep breath. Then he pushed the door open.

Marjorie screamed.

Doons stared. His sphincter let go. He began to whimper.

He saw naked corpses on the floor, some lying on their backs, others sitting with their backs to the far wall. Mutilated. A couple of small boys. A man he didn't recognize. Glendon Morley. An old woman with red pulp where her face should be. Two younger women. One was Thelma. She lay near the door, her torso slit open, a lighted candle imbedded in the coils of her exposed guts, another in her mouth, another protruding from between her legs. Every corpse held a candle in its mouth. Each woman had one in her vagina.

The gorilla stepped out from behind the door.

Still screaming, Marjorie ran up the hall.

Doons swung the hatchet, missed the gorilla by a yard, and ran.

36

Karen Bennett saw them walking along the shoulder of Oakhurst Road. Nate wore a big shirt. His legs were bare below its hanging tails. Bill wore pants, but no shirt. He hugged his chest as he walked.

She stopped beside them, leaned across the passenger seat, and rolled down the window. 'How about a lift?'

'Miss Bennett?' Bill asked.

'None other.' She unlocked the back door. The boys ran to it and climbed in.

'Ah, warmth,' Nate said.

Bill sighed.

'Can I take you fellows home?'

'We're going to the Sherwood house.'

'We're gonna fix their asses.'

'Besides, they've got our stuff.'

'Where'd you get the clothes?'

'Offa the scarecrow. Christ, I think my dick's got frostbite.'

'Nate!' Bill snapped.

'So sorry.'

'Did you come back just for us?' Bill asked.

'Couldn't leave you out in the cold, bare-ass and bleeding.'

Nate laughed. 'Hey, you're a decent lady. Who'd ever think you're a teacher?'

'Anyway, I gót rid of Carlson, the s.o.b., and decided to come looking for you.'

'Did you call the cops?'

She shook her bead. 'They would've been tough on you guys. I figured you'd been through enough without that.'

'Hey hey hey!'

'You really want me to take you to the Sherwood house?'

'Damn right.'

'Dressed like that?'

'It's nothing they haven't already seen, the shit-eaters.'

'Nate.'

'Sorry. Hey Miss Bennett, you wouldn't have a tire iron in your trunk?'

'I may be decent, but I'm not about to provide you with a deadly weapon.' She started driving. 'I'll go in with you, though. Maybe we can get back your things without resorting to...'

'You better not,' Nate said. 'What we're gonna do to those piss-buckets won't be fit for a lady's eyes.'

37

Eric stayed near the front door, and watched the others start up the stairs. They all had candles. They made him think of a peasant mob in a Frankenstein movie.

Doons and his wife rushed down the stairs toward the group. 'Move it!' Doons yelled. 'Move it! There's a killer! Bodies! Oh my God, the bodies! Get down!'

He looked over his shoulder and gasped.

Eric looked. He saw a gorilla in the darkness at the top of the stairs.

Doons shoved his wife. She bumped into Aleshia, and Aleshia stumbled backwards against Eddie. They both fell into those below them. Doons, holding a hatchet high, made his way down through the sprawling teenagers. He pulled his wife along behind him. At the foot of the stairs, he shoved Eric aside and lunged for the door. He gripped the knob, twisted it, jerked. The door hit the latch and banged shut. 'A lock! Who locked the fuckin' door!'

'Eric,' said Miss Major.

Doons swung around. 'Bastard! Give me the key!'

Eric shook his head. 'Nobody leaves.'

Doons raised the hatchet. A shot blasted through the

shouting. A hole appeared in Doons's forehead and a red mass splashed the door. Screams erupted. He fell.

Dropping beside him, Eric grabbed the hatchet. He leaped to his feet.

Mark Bailey reached for him. A shot sent his helmet liner spinning away, and he dropped.

Eric looked at the stairs. The gorilla stood in darkness at the top, the furry suit half off and hanging around his legs. He wore a stained uniform. He held a revolver in both hands. He fired. Eddie Ryker's throat opened.

He fired. The Indian clutched his chest and tumbled backwards.

John the vampire ran past Eric, cape fluttering. A shot exploded. His head jerked forward and he fell sprawling.

The girls kept screaming and wailing. Except for Aleshia. She shouted, 'Run! Run!' She rushed past Eric, and up the hallway beside the stairs. Beth followed her. Then Miss Major, and Mary Lou, and finally Sue Diamond. Only Mrs Doons remained. She lay on the floor, holding her dead husband.

The gorilla kicked free of his suit and came down the stairs, loading his revolver.

'Use the hatchet,' he said, his voice muffled by the black gorilla head. 'Finish her.'

'Dad,' Eric muttered. 'Dad, you ... you weren't supposed to ... you *killed* them!'

'They're your enemies.'

'You weren't supposed to *kill* them!'

'Give me that.' He snatched the hatchet away from Eric. He went to Mrs Doons.

'No!' Eric cried.

'Shut up.'

Mrs Doons didn't look up. He split the back of her head.

'Let's get the others.'

'No.'

He holstered the revolver, and clutched a lapel of Eric's jacket. 'Don't snivel and whine. It's their night to snivel and whine. It's their night to pay for all the times they pissed on you.'

The side of the hatchet head pressed against Eric's pants, rubbed his penis.

'We're gonna fuck 'em. You want to fuck 'em, don't you? We're gonna fuck 'em all, and chop 'em up.'

Eric felt himself getting hard. 'I don't want to kill them.'

'Want 'em to tell? Wanta go to prison? I been there, been fourteen years – long as you been alive, almost. Know how I got there? Somebody told. Out in California. I slit her open but she didn't die like the others, and she told. Can't let 'em tell. Gotta chop 'em up.'

The hatchet went away. A hand touched him through his pants.

'First we're gonna fuck 'em.'

Eric stared at the face of the gorilla. The hand stroked the length of his erection.

'You'll like that, won't you?'

Eric nodded.

'When we're done, I've got a surprise for you. The best surprise of all.'

'Okay.'

He took a flashlight from his pocket. 'Come on.'

* * *

'Elmer,' groaned a low, quiet voice.

Elmer, under the table in the main room, curled closer to the transister radio. It was a large radio, but too small to conceal all of him. He tucked his legs against his belly.

'Elmer?' the voice called. It sounded weak.

He trembled.

He'd thought he was alone in the big, candlelit room.

'Elmer, help me.'

My God, he thought. The gorilla! The voice came from one of the hanging gorillas! He wanted to scurry from under the table and run. But where could he run to? That little shit Eric had padlocked the front door. The rear door, if he could find it, was probably also locked.

To find it, he would have to wander through the dark house. The gorilla with the pistol was out there.

'Elmer.' The voice was stronger now. 'Get out from under the goddamn table and help me.'

The voice, though muffled, sounded vaguely familiar.

Elmer got to his hands and knees. He crawled out from under the table, and gazed up at the nearest gorilla. Its thick, hairy legs were swinging. The other gorilla remained motionless.

'Get your ass in gear and cut me down.'

'Sam?' Elmer whispered.

'Do it!'

Elmer nodded. He turned to the liquor table and picked up a bottle of bourbon. He hated to break it – the noise. Looking around, he saw a heap of clothing on the floor. He rushed to it, tossed aside a vest and striped T-shirt. Hanging from the rope belts of the cut-off jeans were two big knives. He slipped them out of their sheaths and hurried to the window. He looked up at the black gorilla. 'You're too high.'

'Climb the bars.'

'I don't know if I can.'

'You'd better give it the best try of your life.'

They found Sue Diamond curled in the corner of a hallway closet. She whimpered and covered her face as the flashlight shined in her eyes. 'Hold the light.'

Eric took the flashlight.

His father grabbed Sue's feet and dragged her from the closet. She kicked her feet free. She started to sit up. He kicked her in the face and she fell. The back of her head smacked the floor. She didn't move.

He knelt beside her and jerked down the zipper of her jumpsuit. It stopped at her groin. She wore black, lacy panties. He pulled open the jumpsuit, and Eric stared at her big, pale breasts. They jiggled as his father peeled the jumpsuit off her shoulders and down her back. The nipples looked smooth and pink, but they didn't stick out as Eric would have liked.

His father tugged the cuffs, pulling the jumpsuit down her legs and off. He tore off her panties. Eric stared at the curly black tuft of hair.

'Go ahead, she's all yours.'

He ached, but he hesitated.

'Go ahead.'

'What about the others?'

'They're not going anyplace.'

'Can't I wait?'

'Suit yourself.' He handed the hatchet to Eric. Then he knelt between Sue's legs and opened his pants. 'I'll warm her up for you,' he said. He laughed quietly inside the gorilla head, and grabbed her breasts.

Grunting and moaning, Elmer tried to pull himself up the bars. Sweat dripped into his eyes. He tried to find a toe hold in the wall, but his feet slipped down. He let go. 'I can't ... can't make it.'

'Bring over the table. Stand on the table.'

'Yeah!' He rushed to the table. It was laden with a dozen bottles, and two big plastic bags of ice. He lifted one end of the table, and pulled. Its far legs skidded and squawked on the hardwood floor. The table vibrated. The bottles shook and clattered together. One tipped. Elmer gasped and held the table motionless, but it fell. It burst on the floor.

'Oh Christ oh Christ,' he muttered. 'Now we're in for it!'

'Get that table over here!'

'I'll take the things off.' He set it down and reached for the two nearest bottles.

'It'll take too long. Don't. Just ... just get it over here and cut me down.'

Elmer moaned. He looked toward the foyer, then around at the closed door to the rear.

'Hurry!'

He picked up the end of the table and again began to drag it toward the window. The bottles swayed and clinked. Another fell and exploded, but Elmer didn't stop.

* * *

'What was that?' Eric said.

'Who cares?' His father climbed off Sue Diamond. 'Your turn.'

'I don't want to.'

'Why not?'

'I want to wait.'

'What for?'

'Aleshia. The ballerina.'

His father nodded. He held out a hand. Eric gave him the hatchet. 'Watch this.'

Eric tried to watch. At the last moment, he shut his eyes. He heard a wet thud, and splashing sounds. More thuds.

'Let's go.'

Eric looked down. Sue Diamond's white skin was shiny with blood. She no longer had a head.

His father hurled it down the hallway. It vanished into the darkness, trailing black hair. A moment later, it crashed against something. It thumped once more, and was quiet.

They walked up the hallway.

The head lay near a shut door, looking up at them. The nose was smashed almost flat. Most of the front teeth were gone. The door had a red smear where the head struck it.

Eric stepped around the head.

His father stepped over it and pushed the door. As it swung open, Eric heard a quiet gasp from inside the kitchen.

They stepped in.

He swung the flashlight. Its beam lit the door to the

back porch, safely padlocked shut on the inside. It shined on the linoleum floor, on cupboards and a sink, on a white-painted wooden door.

'The utility closet.' His father laughed softly.

They walked toward the closet door, and Eric's father jerked it open.

Aleshia sprang out at him. He drove a knee into her belly, the impact lifting her feet off the floor. She fell facedown.

'This Aleshia?'

'Yeah.'

'The one you want?'

'Yeah.'

'Know what's funny?'

'What?'

'This is where I got Hester. Right here. Right where you're gonna get Aleshia.'

'Who's Hester?'

'Hester Sherwood. Lived here a long time ago. This is where I fucked her. Right here.' He rolled Aleshia over. Eric shined the flashlight on her. She was grimacing, gasping for air, clutching her belly. 'Right here on the floor.' He ripped her bodice down.

Standing on the table, Elmer sawed through the rope that bound Sam's right hand to the upper crossbar. When the rope parted, Sam's arm flopped down as if lifeless.

'How'd you get here?' Elmer asked, starting on the other rope.

'Crashed. My head...'

'You've been unconscious?'

The gorilla head nodded. 'I heard shots. Guess they brought me out of it. I saw you come running in.'

Elmer grabbed one of the bars, pressed himself against Sam, and cut through the rope. Sam's arm dropped. Elmer used all his strength to force him against the bars, but it wasn't enough. Sam's heels slid over the table top, pushed through bottles, knocked them to the floor. Then he was sitting on the table, straddled by Elmer. Elmer climbed off and jumped to the floor.

Sam continued to sit on the table.

'Now what?' Elmer asked.

'Help me to my feet.'

'Want her?'

Eric swallowed. He stared at Aleshia's small, pale breasts. The nipples stood rigid. 'Yeah,' he said.

His father tugged Aleshia's tutu down her legs. He peeled down her tights.

Off to the side, a cupboard door squeaked open. Eric swung the flashlight. In its beam he saw Beth. She climbed from the cupboard and stood up.

'Get out of here, Beth,' Eric said.

Her eyes widened and gazed at him with a dull stare. Her mouth dropped open. Her head tilted to one side, and she moaned.

'Beth.'

She staggered toward him.

'What the fuck is she doing?'

Eric shook his head.

His father gave him the hatchet. 'Chop her down.'

She shambled forward as if in a daze. Her face was

streaked with burnt cork, smeared with Vampire Blood. Her thigh showed through the tear in her dress, and Eric remembered how she'd ripped her clothes to better look the part.

Her arm went behind Eric's back. He felt the pressure of her breasts against his chest.

'Chop her.'

He felt her warm breath on the side of his neck. Then her teeth. They bit into his neck and ripped. He shrieked. Beth jerked the hatchet from his hand and shoved him backwards.

Spitting Eric's blood and flesh, Beth lunged at the man in the gorilla head. She swung the hatchet, but he caught her arm and took it away. Roaring, he flung her to the floor. He raised the hatchet high.

Something huge and dark ran at him from the kitchen door. He turned, swinging the hatchet. It hacked into the dark thing's arm, and she heard a grunt of pain. But the dark thing – a gorilla – didn't stop. It smashed against the man and plunged a knife into his belly.

Screaming, he shoved the gorilla. It stumbled over Aleshia and fell. He pulled the knife from his belly. Threw it down. Raised the hatchet and stumbled toward the gorilla.

Beth crawled for the knife.

He kicked her in the side and she tumbled over, gasping.

The door from the back porch crashed open.

'That asshole's got an ax!'

'Oh shit!'

'Drop it!'

He turned toward Nate and Bill.

'Back off, monkey-face! I'm warning you!'

He staggered toward them.

Bill saw a knife on the floor. He dived for it, grabbed it, flung it toward Nate and rolled against the man's feet.

The man fell backwards, growling.

Nate leaped over Bill. His knees drove into the man's belly. The man screeched. Nate pressed the knife to his throat.

'Who is this fuck-head?' he said.

'Kill him,' said a girl.

'Beth?' Bill asked.

'Kill him.'

'Not me,' Nate said. 'I may be a shit, but I'm not a killer.'

Epilogue

'He died in surgery.'

'What a shame.'

'Yeah. My heart bleeds. He should've been executed for the California murders, but they didn't have capital punishment back then. So he got life. Which came down to fourteen years and a massacre in Ashburg.'

'He won't kill anyone else.'

Sam nodded

'He murdered Clara Hayes and all the Horners so they wouldn't interrupt his party?'

'And because he enjoyed it, I suppose.'

'You didn't say, though. What about the third gorilla?'

'Cynthia.'

'Oh my God.'

'She was dead. He must've got her ... I don't know, sometime that afternoon.'

'I'm sorry, Sam.'

'Well...'

Melodie lay her head against Sam's chest, and they sat in silence for a long time in her room behind the office of the Sleepy Hollow Inn.